T0157705

# CHANCE ENCOUNTERS

# CHANCE ENCOUNTERS

*Shattered Hope Restored*

Margaret Conger

# CHANCE ENCOUNTERS
## SHATTERED HOPE RESTORED

*Holy Bible, New International Version®, NIV® Copyright ©1973, 1978, 1984, 2011 by Biblica, Inc.® Used by permission. All rights reserved worldwide.*

*Scripture taken from the New King James Version®. Copyright © 1982 by Thomas Nelson. Used by permission. All rights reserved.*

*iUniverse books may be ordered through booksellers or by contacting:*

*iUniverse*
*1663 Liberty Drive*
*Bloomington, IN 47403*
*www.iuniverse.com*
*1-800-Authors (1-800-288-4677)*

*ISBN: 978-1-5320-8166-8 (sc)*
*ISBN: 978-1-5320-8167-5 (e)*

*Library of Congress Control Number: 2019912979*

*Print information available on the last page.*

*iUniverse rev. date: 09/18/2019*

# CHAPTER 1

# Escape

Sophie was at the end of a line of prisoners as they marched back to the Birkenau camp, a part of the Auschwitz prison camp. The wind was howling in their faces and made each step more difficult than the last one. She began to doubt that she had she energy to continue the march back to camp. On this late November day darkness came early and snow was beginning to fall making it difficult to see more than a few feet ahead. They had spent the day moving stone from a pit to a place where a road was to be built.

Sophie was tired from the days work and had so little to eat that she doubted that she had could keep walking. She kept her face buried in the collar of her coat trying to cut the effects of the biting wind but it really was not helping. Each step was worse than the one before.

The group of prisoners had lost all sense of an orderly march. It was impossible to stay aside each other in the prescribed five to a row order. It was each person struggling to stay upright as we moved along the narrow track next to the woods. The guards were having as much trouble as we prisoners were. They had fallen way back almost out of sight.

The walk from the stone pit where they had been working that day was five miles from camp. Sophie was exhausted from moving stone all day and kept thinking about the sign hanging at the gate of the prison camp *"arbeit macht frei"* (work makes you free). We prisoners knew that the only way to get free from this torture was death. Was this my day to die? Should I try to keep going? But what about my husband Jake? I had no news of him since he left to fight in the Polish army three years ago. Was he still alive somewhere or had he died? At times I had no hope of ever seeing him again. But what if somehow he survived and I gave up? No, I just had to keep going; somehow I would make it!

We had been given a piece of dry bread and what passed as a thin soup at noon today. But by now that little amount of food was not enough to keep me from feeling faint. I had kept some of the bread in my pocket to eat later in case we were late getting back to camp and had missed the evening meal as happened yesterday. If Eliza had not saved me some of her evening soup, I would have had nothing to eat last evening after a long day moving stone.

I had been a prisoner at Auschwitz for six months now. Up until yesterday I had been working indoors in the kitchen. There it was possible to secrete a scrap of food that I could hide under my dress that I would take back to the barracks to share with Eliza, my friend from Krakow. We had known each other since our elementary school days. We were both captured and sent to Auschwitz at the same time. Eliza was the last person I had to hold onto. My father had been sent to a work camp a year earlier; my mother died of what I think was a broken heart. I often wondered why I was still struggling to stay alive. Was there any hope for us? If it were not for Eliza, I would have given up. She kept telling me that we could survive this! Her courage was what was keeping me going. But working in the stone pit was more than I could endure. And with this weather I knew that I would not survive much longer.

Eliza had been assigned to work in the clothing room at the camp sorting clothes confiscated from the prisoners on their arrival at the camp. Yesterday she had hidden a heavy wool sweater under her dress and brought it back to our barracks. She insisted that I wear it today under my dress where I could keep it hidden by the thin coat we had been issued in the morning. Working out doors as it was getting colder was almost more than I could survive and the extra warmth was wonderful. The coat itself would not have been much help against the biting wind.

The uneven path made walking difficult. I suddenly lost my balance, tripped, and rolled down the embankment into a ditch hitting my head on a stone. For several moments I lay there not sure what had happened. I expected that at any moment the guards would spot me and shout for me to get up and keep walking. Or was this the end? Would they just shoot me? But nothing happened. No one noticed me. I don't know how long I was there but finally realized that I was alone. The guards had passed me by without realizing I was lying in the ditch. They too were struggling just to keep moving forward. With their heads down and buried into their coats they had not noticed me lying there.

Was this a chance to escape? I knew that I would be missed at roll call that evening. Or I might even be missed as we went back through the gate to the prison. Staying here in the ditch along the road was not an option. I struggled to climb out of the ditch and then headed into the woods with no idea where I was going. Just going! Away! The night was so dark that it was hard to see ahead of me. But at least in the woods the wind was not as fierce as it had been out in the open.

I don't know how long I walked or in what direction I was going. I knew it was away from the stone pit where we had been working but without stars or moon to guide me I had no sense of direction. All I knew was that each step took me farther from road we had been on. The trees here were large and tightly spaced. I was able to move among them more easily because there was not much undergrowth. But the snow was beginning to fall more steadily now.

Walking was becoming more difficult. I stumbled several times but was able to catch my self by grabbing onto the nearest tree. I don't know how long I had been walking. I was so tired that I didn't think I could go any further. But lying down here in the open would be deadly. Just then I stumbled onto a very large old tree that had the center hollowed out. I was able to crawl into the opening and found it large enough to sit down. Inside this tree cave I was out of the wind and snow. As I huddled into my coat and sweater I was less cold than I had been for hours. The tree was providing the shelter that I needed. I pulled the sweater down as far as it could reach and pulled my legs up so they were partly covered by the sweater. But my hunger and thirst were devastating. I reached down to the cup tied to my dress and filled it with some snow and warmed it under my sweater. With the water and the bread from my pocket my thirst was quenched and the hunger pains were less.

I don't know how long I sat there before falling asleep. But when I woke up it was getting light outside. The snow was quite deep closing off part of the entrance to my shelter and helped to keep my space warmer. With the little bit of light flittering in, I began to explore where I was. Right behind where I was sitting was a large pile of pine nuts – did some squirrel hide them here? I was able to crack a few open with two stones found on the ground,. Along with some snow that I melted under my sweater my meal was provided. I thought about how God had fed the Israelite's with manna from heaven and water from the rock. Was this my manna? Was it possible that God was providing for me? After years of abuse by the Germans was there hope for escape?

I was sure that my absence had already been detected and a search had begun. It would go on for three days. There must already be dogs out as part of the search but with the new snowfall they would not be very effective. My chance of being found here was getting less so I realized trying to move out was not a good idea. With the snow on the ground any tracks I made would be easily found. So I was trapped in my shelter for at least 3 days or even longer if the snow was too deep to move out. I counted the nuts that were in the pile – only 25 of them.

These would have to be carefully rationed out to last the 3 days that I would have to stay here.

During that day and night I drifted in and out of sleep. I could hear dogs barking in the distance but they never came near because the deep snow kept them from picking up my scent. My thought went back to my family. Was my father still alive somewhere? Where was Jake my husband? I was too cold and tired to concentrate on prayer, but I just kept saying, "God help me. I don't know what to do".

The cold of the night was almost unbearable even as I wrapped up in the heavy sweater and tried to make myself as small as possible. My whole body ached from the tight position I had to stay in. But it was warmer than the cold barracks back at the camp. Yet I missed not having Eliza with me. We had been inseparable since we were forced into the ghetto back in Krakow. Our families were gone and we had become almost like sisters. The day we were forced by the German soldiers to leave the ghetto and board the cattle car for the ride to Auschwitz we managed to stay together. At the camp we also managed to stay together; but now we were separated. Why God is this happening to me? Is there no one in the world who cares about me? My prayers for help are unanswered.

As I hid in my tree cave my thoughts went back to all that had happened since this war began. I remembered my grief when we got the notice that Jake, my husband, had to report to the Polish Army. I have had no news of him since the day he left. No one seemed to know what happened to army recruits. We had heard about the Germans killing many of the officers. Did they also kill the troops? Or was Jake in the East where the Russians were in control? Was he still alive? Probably not, but I prayed for his safety anyway. I thought about Eliza who would be so worried about me. And I thought about my home back in Krakow. Would I ever see it again? What should I do now? I had no escape plan!

# CHAPTER 2

# The Search

It seemed to Eliza that the morning roll call at the barracks went on forever. We were standing there in the falling snow almost too cold to endure. Our Kapo counted us over and over again. Sophie was missing. She had not returned from her work detail last evening. I talked with some of the others in her work group but they had no idea what could have happened to her; they told me how difficult it was to walk in the storm and they had lost track of each other. Did she fall down and no one noticed her. Had she been shot? All I knew was that she had not returned last evening. And now the Kapo was going to find out that she was missing.

The Kapo called out each of our numbers trying to find out who was missing. I knew that Sophie was the missing person, but I would not be the one to report her. Finally the Kapo realized Sophie was not there. She ordered a search of the barracks but of course Sophie was not there. We were discharged back to the barracks and given our morning meal while the Kapo went to report Sophie's absence. There would be no work details today while a search was underway. We sat on our beds talking about what could have happened to her. The girls on her work detail were of no help. They knew that she was with them as they started back to camp. But as the weather became worse they were all having trouble walking. Even the guards seemed to pay less attention to them than usual. So Sophie's disappearance remained a mystery.

The sirens started to blow alerting all of us that a search was underway. The guards assigned to yesterday's work detail at the stone pit were called in for questioning but they were not much help. They insisted that when they returned to camp last evening they had counted the prisoners and all were accounted for. They were sure that the prisoner had returned to camp. This started a search of the entire camp. At the same time a search detail with the dogs set out from camp to follow the road looking to see if any trace of the prisoner could be found.

The sirens from the camp were heard for several miles around the country side. At the Convent of the Sacred Heart, Sister Anna heard the sirens and knew that someone had escaped from the prison camp. She called the sisters together and asked for prayer for the missing person. Why were these Germans so concerned about one person. If the prisoner was found she knew that the outcome would be death. She had come to hate being so close to the death camp where the smell of the burning bodies never left. "Why God am I here? Will this horror never end?"

Sister Anna did not have long to wait to hear about the escaped prisoner. She saw the prison camp guard's car pull in at the convent and two soldiers jumped out. They rushed into the convent hallway and demanded to see the "person in charge". Sister met them and asked what they wanted. They said "there's a prisoner who has escaped from our work camp and we must find her. In this weather she could be in great harm. Have you seen any stranger in the area?" Sister Anna said "no, we know nothing about this." "Well we need to search this place. How do we know you're not lying. Call all of your nuns and staff here so we can question everyone." The soldiers shouted at them in very broken Polish but learned nothing new. The nuns and the staff knew no more about the missing person than did Sister Anna.

Frustrated with their interrogation, they said "we are searching everywhere. If you are lying, the consequences will be severe." With that they rushed down the hallway and began the search. They broke into every room, even areas that we considered private. They searched behind the drapes in the chapel; they searched in the pantry of the kitchen. They even searched in the wood shed. The search was fruitless! As they came back to the doorway they reminded Sister Anna that there was a 500 zloty reward for turning a prisoner over to them and let them know if she saw anyone suspicious in the area. With that they were off just as quickly as they had come.

Sister Anna called everyone back into the chapel to pray for the missing young woman. But there was little else that she could do. That night sleep did not come to her. Suddenly she had a thought – the old tree with the hollowed out opening. Could it be possible that the prisoner had found it. Had God given her a message? Was this the reason she was placed so close to the death camp? This was the question she had had for several years. What if God had a purpose for her being here?

The next morning Sister Anna called Pietre, the convent handy man, into her office. "What do you know about the search for the missing prisoner? Have they found anything?" "No, they're still searching but it seems the search is going farther away from here" replied Pietre." Sister Anna said "Well, God has given me a message. Perhaps we can help protect this poor young woman." "What are you talking about? We don't know anything about her or where she might be" Pietre exclaimed. "All I know is that the Germans have not found her yet."

"Would you be willing to do something for me" asked Sister Anna. "I want you to take the sleigh and go into the forest to cut some wood. I had a vision last night that she might be hiding in the old tree with the hallowed out center. Go to the woods for the day with the sleigh and cut up some wood. Before coming back, check the old tree. I know this sounds strange, but God has given me this feeling that she may be out there and needs our help. Can I trust you to help her if you find her?"

Pietre was stunned with Sister Anna's request. He knew that any attempt to help an escaped prisoner would cost his life if the Germans found him with her. But he hated the German occupation of Poland so much! His only son had been killed early in the war. And he hated what he and the others in the area knew about the death camp. And besides, what was the chance that Sister Anna's vision was really true. But at the same time he had worked with Sister Anna now for many years and he knew that she was a person who lived close to God. Perhaps there was a purpose for him in this affair. "Yes, Sister Anna, I'll go. Do you want me to bring her here if I find her?" "Of course" replied Sister Anna. "We'll have to find a way to protect her if God leads you to her."

Pietre started out with the sleigh and an ax to go search in the woods. As he was cutting up branches from a fallen tree, another detail of Germans with their dogs rushed up to him. "What are you doing old man" they asked. "Just collecting firewood. The snow is making it possible to get into the woods." The dogs sniffed around the sleigh but found nothing. "Well there's a missing prisoner. There is a big reward for turning her in if you see her." With disgust the Germans took off continuing their search along the road.

Pietre stared at them as they moved off. "Help you – I guess not." I waited until they were long out of sight before I went further into the forest.

I continued collecting wood farther into the forest until late afternoon. As dusk was approaching I brought the sleigh with its load of wood towards the old tree that Sister Anna had asked that I check. I saw that the opening was partly covered with snow. I quietly called into the opening – "Is anyone here?"

Sophie heard someone coming towards her hiding place and was petrified. Was this the end for her? She sank farther back into the opening and prayed that she would not be found. But then she heard the voice saying "I'm here to help you. Sister Anna has sent me to bring you to the convent." Sophie heard the Polish words and realized it was not the German guards who had found her.

Pietre took his shovel and began clearing the snow away from the opening. As he looked into the opening he saw a person crouching in the back of the tree cave. "Please come out, I'm here to take you to safety." He knelt down and helped Sophie slide towards the opening and then picked her up and carried her to the sleigh. There he wrapped her in a blanket. "Here, down under the wood in this opening you will be safe." Pietre then covered the load of wood with an old blanket. Sophie was so afraid, cold and tired that she was not able to respond. Who was this person? Would he really help her? Who was Sister Anna? How could she know where I had been hiding? Should she try to run? But running was not an option. She knew she had no place to go.

Before leaving the area, Pietre stomped around the whole area leaving large boot prints everywhere and covered the opening into the tree with snow. If the Germans come back here they will not suspect anything. They will see the large footprints, remember they had met me earlier in the day and not connect the footprints with their escaped prisoner. Besides my footprints were big – not the footprints of the woman they were looking for.

It was getting dark by the time Pietre and Sophie set off for the convent. They moved out onto the road and joined the many tracks left by the German search party. There would be no way to know that the sleigh had come this way. Fortunately they met no one along the road.

As they came up to the convent yard, Pietre told Sophie to stay hidden until it was safe to move her into the convent. He went in through the kitchen and told the cook to get Sister Anna quickly. When Sister Anna arrived, he told her "I found the girl. You were right. She was in the old tree cave." Under the cover of darkness Pietre carried Sophie into the convent and put her in a bed in a small room off the kitchen. Sister Anna quickly brought some hot tea and soup and helped Sophie sit up to eat. She had the cook warm some stones to place in the bed under Sophie. "I want you to rest now and get warm. Tomorrow we will find a better hiding place for you."

# CHAPTER 3

# The Convent

Sophie slept fitfully that night trying to get warm after being in the cold for so long. The warm stones helped at first, but then got cold. The room she was in was dark – no windows. She had so many questions. Where was she? Should she try to escape? Who were these people who had found her? What would happen now? Was this just a way for someone to turn her in for a reward? Or was God hearing her prayers for help? But at the moment she was safe. She spent the night in prayer.

Sister Anna was also having a fitful night. What was she doing? Why was she endangering the life of everyone in the convent by protecting this prisoner? She had never done anything like this before. What had made her get involved?

*And the king shall answer and say unto them, Verily I say unto you, in as much as you have done it unto one of*

> *the least of these my brethren, ye have done it unto me*
> *Matthew 25:40 (KJV)*

These words rang in her – visit the prisoner, give food to the hungry, give water to the thirsty. She was serving God. The months of smelling the burning flesh from the prison camp, the anger she had felt about innocent people being rounded up as cattle, the horrors of this war had brought her to this point. Now was her chance to do something however so small. This was the message she was given and needed to share it with her fellow nuns. Here was our opportunity to serve God! We must take the opportunity given to us to help even if it was only one person.

At day break there was a knock at Sophie's door. It was Sister Anna with some hot tea and bread and cheese. Real food! Not the hard stale bread Sophie had become accustomed to at the camp. It was also more than she had when living in the ghetto. Was this Heaven? Sister Anna said "After you eat, we have a warm bath ready for you and some clean clothes. Then we have to get you into a safer hiding place for a few days until the guards stop looking for you. We must be prepared in case they come back to search again."

With a hurried bath and new clothes, I felt the cleanest I had been since the day we were forced into the ghetto in Krakow. I didn't even ask where my prison dress was but Sister Anna told me that they had burned it in the stove. "Don't worry, we would not keep that around." Sister Anna then led me from the kitchen area into the convent chapel. Behind the altar area was a door covered by a large painting that led to a small closet. Inside was a chair and several blankets to cover up with. Sister Anna told me that I needed to stay here for several days but she would bring food and a chamber pot. She told me that when the German guards had searched the convent several days ago, they had not found this room. "It should be safe for you. We'll be close by. Please just stay here until we know that the search for you is over."

Who were these people? I knew that if they were found helping a Jew they too would be put in prison or killed. Yet they were my protectors. How could this be? My experience with Catholics in the past had not been good. Could I really trust Sister Anna? Yet she seemed to be doing everything to keep me safe. Growing up I had had some contact with nuns at the school in our town. They had never paid much attention to the Jewish kids. But these nuns seemed different. I would have to ask Sister Anna some time why she seemed so intent on helping me.

The day passed slowly but I was warm under the blankets. The room was dark but a slit of light came in under the door. In that way I was able to tell the difference between night and day. I began to pay attention to the sounds coming from the chapel. The nuns were there several times that day. I heard their singing and prayers. Just hearing their voices was making me feel less alone.

Several days went by with the same pattern. Three times a day Sister Anna would arrive with food – never very much but very welcome. The soup was thick with vegetables and some meat. The bread was fresh. The tea was warm. This was more food than I had had in many months. I waited with anticipation for the times the nuns would come to the chapel to pray and sing. Did they know I was here? Or was this just known to Sister Anna, Pietre, and the cook. I asked Sister Anna why she was doing this. And how did she know where I was hiding in that tree. She replied that she would tell me more when it was safe for her to spend more time with me.

I gradually began to pray along with the nuns thanking God for my rescue, a safe hiding place, and food. And every day Sister Anna would tell me about the search. It seemed that the guards were searching farther away from the area. The people in the community thought that the guards were sure that someone had picked me up and taken me back to Krakow. Others thought that my body would be found when the snow melted. At any rate they had not come back to the convent to search.

## Sister Anna's Plan

Sister Anna left the chapel quickly when she got word that Father Aloysius was here to see her. She hurried to her office to meet him and

15

hear what he knew about the search. He looked very troubled when we met. "How is the search going "I asked? "No news yet", he replied. "These bastards are just relentless in looking for just one innocent person. Sorry about the language. I don't know how much longer I can stand to live under these people." I had never heard him use such language. He told me that the search was moving away from our area and that most people believed that the prisoner had in some way met up with the partisans in the area. He then asked about how the sisters were doing and how they had reacted to the search of the convent by the German guards. I was not sure what to tell him. Could he be trusted with my secret?

I told him about the sister's reaction to the search of the convent. At first they were frightened, then they became very angry. I asked him what he would do if he somehow found the prisoner. "That is hardly a question," he replied. "I would find someway to hide her. There's no way that I would turn her over to those thugs or take their money for her capture. We have our first responsibility to God to care for those in trouble. Why do you ask? Is there something we should talk about?"

"Father, I have something to tell you. The prisoner is here. She is hidden here in the convent." "What! How can this be? Are you telling me that you have her hidden here?" So I told Father Aloysius about my vision from God about the old tree and how she may have found refuge there. How Pietre had gone looking and brought her here. Now we needed to plan how to keep her hidden. Sister Anna said. "I would like to keep her hidden as one of the sisters. She could wear the convent dress and be hidden in plain sight here in the convent." "Whew, I need to think about this" Father replied. "How do we explain the presence of a new person? You can't just have someone new show up. People would be very suspicious." We talked about several ideas but none of them seemed to be workable. Was it best to keep her hidden away from others in the convent? Or was the idea of being in a public area the best move. Finally Father Aloysius said "Wait, I have an idea. The convent that my niece lived at has been bombed and the nuns all had to leave. I could put out the word that I have brought my niece here to give her shelter. That would explain the addition of a new person."

"What about the deceit of pretending our Jewish prisoner is a Catholic nun? Can God forgive us for lying about this?" asked Sister Anna. Father replied "I think that is the least of our worries. Remember when the Lutherans did something similar? When Martin Luther was under threat by Charles V, the Holy Roman Emperor, he was hidden in Wartburg Castle pretending to be Junker George, a knight. If the Lutherans could do it, why can't we? God did not rain down fire and brimstone on them. Sometimes we have to live differently when we're in evil times."

So we continued to plan how to carry out the prisoner's introduction to the convent. First we had to meet with all of the sisters to talk about the plan and the danger it put all of us in. Only if they all agreed would we keep our prisoner here. If not, we would have to find another hiding place. They would all have to agree to take the risk. If she were found here we could all face death. What was my responsibility to the other nuns. Could I put them in such danger?

Sister Anna called all of the nuns together in the chapel. She opened the prayer time with reading from Matthew chapter 25. "God has laid this passage on my heart.

> *"for I was hungry and you gave me food, I was thirsty and you gave me something to drink, and I was a stranger and you welcomed me, I was naked and you gave clothing, I was sick and you took care of me, I was in prison and you visited me."* Matthew 25:35-36.(NIV)

*Sister Anna continued* "we need to consider what are the implications of this lesson for us today. Who is the stranger in our midst? What would God have us do? You all know that a prisoner has escaped from the camp. Several days ago God gave me a vision about where her hiding place might be. We found her and brought her here. "She went on to explain how God had given her the message that our way to serve God was to protect the poor, the prisoner, the hungry. "You all know the consequences for aiding a Jew. Each of you must take time in prayer to consider whether you are willing to help to protect this innocent young woman. Consider the danger that her presence here pus all of in." There was silence in the room. Then one by one each of the nuns agreed to be a part of the plan. They had many questions about what would be done. But they all agreed to accept the prisoner as one of them and do whatever was needed.

# Sophie

I was getting tired of hiding in the closet but I knew that it was best to stay here. I had heard the discussion among the sisters about the plan to hide me as a nun here in the convent. So I just needed to wait until Sister Anna thought it safe for me to come out of hiding. The next several days went on in the same pattern. The nuns came to the chapel regularly to pray and sing. The light from the chapel filtered into my closet reminding me that time was passing. I lost count of the days.

One morning Sister Anna brought me my food and said that she thought it was now safe for me to come out. Her plan was for me to dress as one of the nuns and blend into the life of the convent. My work assignment was to be in the kitchen where I would be near the safety of the pantry in case anyone came to the convent. The cook had rearranged the barrels of cabbage so they covered over the trap door to the root cellar. In case I needed to hide, I was to run to the pantry and move the barrels and open the trap door. After I went down into the root cellar, the cook would replace the barrels covering over the door. The fall harvest was in and there was a good supply of potatoes and vegetables there. Between the barrels of cabbage and the sacks of potatoes the pantry was very full. It was hard to even see in there.

Sister Anna told me that I was now Sister Gertrude. She had an identity paper that showed that. The picture on it was not very clear, but it would probably pass most inspections. She told me that I was supposed to be the niece of the local priest. I had to learn my story about being bombed out of my convent and having nowhere to go so Father Aloysius had brought me here. I was skeptical about this plan but I had no other choice. I did have confidence in Sister Anna and all she had done thus far to protect me.

She took me back into the convent to a small room where a dress and head covering were laid out. I took another bath and was ready to try on my new clothes. Sister Olga came in to help me put it on. After wearing the prison dress for so long this would take time to get familiar with. It was long and warm. The best part of it was that it completely covered my arm with the hated number tattooed on my skin. I no longer had to look at it. The habit was going to be comfortable in the winter but I wondered about how it would feel in the summer. But that was not my worry today. Perhaps this war would be over by then and the hated Germans chased out of Poland. My bigger worry was if this plan would work. It seemed like I would be hiding in the open!

So a new chapter in my life began. Sister Olga worked in the kitchen along with me. It was her job to teach me how to live life as a nun. She was a patient teacher. She insisted that I learn the Lord's Prayer. She had heard that the German officials' used it as a test when someone was brought in for questioning. They presumed that a Jew would not know it. And she explained about the hours of prayer and why we met in the chapel so many times during the day and night. I remembered that we as Jews also had regular times for prayer.

At first trying to live as a Catholic nun troubled my conscience. Was I being a traitor to my Jewish heritage? But I remembered my parents discussion about eating pork back in the ghetto. My father said "We can eat what God has provided in times like these. We must do what is needed to stay alive. God will forgive us."

Although I did not understand the words used in the chapel – they were in Latin – I found the time there to be soothing. I prayed the prayers that had been said around our dinner table from the time I was a child. I did not understand the God that the others were worshipping, but the love they had shown me was all that I needed.

One morning in the spring I was in the chapel for the Prime (6:AM) devotion. A beam of light suddenly lit up the man on the cross at the front of the chapel. A wave of understanding swept over me. So they killed you also was the thought that overwhelmed me. The hate shown to this Jesus was no different than the hate the Germans had for us Jews. But not everyone held on to this hate. The nuns here in the convent were risking their lives to protect me. The bitterness I had felt for so many months gradually began to leave me and I began to hope that somehow life would once again have some meaning.

# CHAPTER 4

# Freedom

The news about the war was changing. We were hearing gun fire almost everyday. There were reports that the Russian army was close by and the German army was on the run. Pietre, our handyman, also kept us informed about the war in the west from the news he was getting on his radio. The radio, of course, was forbidden by the Germans, but he listened every night anyway. He heard that the allied forces were advancing deeper into Europe. It seemed that the Germans were going to be defeated. So even though our food supplies were getting low and the weather was very cold, we had hope. It seemed that the end of this German occupation would come soon.

It was late in January when Sister Anna called me into her office. "My little Jewish princess, you are now safe to go. The Germans have been forced westward and the Russians are in control. Your days of having to hide are over. I have put together a little package with some food and money to help you get to Krakow. Perhaps there you will be able to find some of your family who have also survived." I was stunned. It had been almost two years since I had been taken as a prisoner to Auschwitz. What would I find back in Krakow- would there be any word of my husband Jake? Was it possible that Eliza had survived as well?

After the safety of the convent for these many months I was afraid to leave. Sister Anna took my hands and said "God will be with you – He has protected you all of this time. He must have something wonderful planned for your future." She then wrapped me in her arms and blessed me.

> *The Lord bless you and keep you:*
> *The Lord make his face shine upon you.*
> *The Lord lift up His countenance upon you*
> *and be gracious unto you. And give you peace.*
> *Numbers 6:24-26 (NKJV).*

How could I thank her for the love she had shown me. She and the other nuns had risked their lives to protect me. There was no way that I could ever repay them for all they had done for me.

I changed into regular clothes and packed a little food in a bag. It was more than five miles to the train station in Oswiecim, but faithful Pietre was waiting for me with the cart and horse. The January day was cold but clear. I looked at the bright blue sky with wonder. It had been so long since I had been outside that the sunshine was almost more than my eyes were able to bear. Was I really free to be out among people again? Did I look like an ordinary Polish woman rather than a Jewish prisoner?

I was overcome with emotion. How could I thank Pietre for his part in rescuing me. Without him I know I would have died in the forest. His bravery in facing certain death if the Germans had found out what he had done was overwhelming to me. I would never forget how he had saved me from that tree cave and brought me to the convent.

Pietre was, as usual, ready with much needed information. His knowledge about the status of the Germans and the camp had always amazed me. He told me that when the Russians had arrived at the prison camp they found a few survivors. Unfortunately most of the prisoners had been sent on a march west along with the retreating Germans. The survivors found at the camp had been taken to hospitals in Krakow. He suggested that was where I could begin to look for any family or friends who had survived.

The ride to the station was frightening because it had been so many years since I had been free to move about. First I was locked in the ghetto. Then I was in the prison camp. Then I was hiding in the forest, and finally in the convent. Did I even know how to act around other people? What did I look like with my hair so short – cut in the convent to make me look like the other nuns. The clothes I was wearing were not my own. They were from Pietre's wife – and made me look like a Polish peasant. If I did find anyone from my past life would they even recognize me? And what about the Russians who were now in control. Would they be any better than the German occupier's? There were so many unknowns.

When we got to the train station Pietre went in to check on the train and buy me a ticket. It was with tremendous fear that I got out of the cart and said good by. He handed me the ticket and told me where to wait for the train. I was thankful that he had gotten the ticket and the information because I was fearful of even talking with an unknown person. Would somebody recognize me as a Jew? Was the hate for Jews really gone? Would someone try to rearrest me?

The train soon arrived. I was part of a large crowd of people all trying to get on at once. Everyone else seemed to know what to do. But for me, I was shaking with fear. But I climbed into the train and found a seat next to two old women. They were busy talking with each other and paid no attention to me.

The trip to Krakow took several hours. But it was more comfortable then when I had been in the cattle car when we were taken to Auschwitz. So much had happened since then! And this time I was all alone. Eliza had been such a comfort on that last journey but now I had no idea where she might be if she was still alive. The thought of facing the future alone was terrifying. But I could not stay in the convent forever. I had to begin finding a way to build a new life!

The countryside looked so different than I had remembered from my childhood. There was destruction everywhere. The people on the train looked thin, their clothes were shabby. The war had been hard on them also. I hardly dared to look at the people around me. Would they recognize me as a Jewish prisoner? The hated number on my arm was well hidden under my coat but was there something about me that just screamed "Jewish prisoner"? I tried to hold on to the words Sister Anna had given me. What was my future?

The train pulled into the main station in Krakow. It looked familiar, there was not much damage from the war. So I had to leave the safety of the train car and head into the unknown. This was the beginning of my new life.

# CHAPTER 5

# Krakow

The city I had known all of my life did not look familiar. Where to begin looking? There was no one on the street where we used to live. In fact all of the streets were empty. The windows in the buildings were broken. It looked like a ghost town. Were people afraid to be out on the streets? Or were there no people left? I went to our synagogue but it also was empty. The doors were tightly locked. There were signs saying keep out. I didn't know where to start looking for any survivors. Was I all alone in the world? A wave of despair almost overwhelmed me. Was I without any hope? Did my survival from the ghetto and the concentration camp just lead me to more despair?

As I wandered away from the old Jewish area, I found a little café open and went in. The woman at the counter looked somewhat familiar. Suddenly I recognized her – she was Maria, our cook before the war. She recognized me at almost the same instant and came running to give me a hug. "Sophie you're alive! Praise God! Here sit down, let me get you a cup of coffee. What has happened to you? How did you get here? I can't believe that you have survived all of this horror." We had so much to tell each other. She told me that after we had been forced into the ghetto she had gone back to our apartment and tried to collect a few of our things. She couldn't get much because the Germans had already looted it but she was able to save some of the silver we had hidden and clothing. We made arrangements for me to meet her after work to pick up some of the things. Real clothes! And perhaps the silver could be sold. It's for sure that I had no need for silver now. She also told me about the Jewish refugee center that was collecting names of survivors as they retuned and urged me to register there. They would also help me find a place to stay and possibly some kind of a job. So once again God was leading me. At least I had someone left from my old life.

I found the Jewish center just off the market square. The building had been badly damaged but still had the outside walls standing. The inside was cavernous because the inside walls were all missing. It showed years of neglect. Along the walls were large papers where a person could write his name in case anyone was searching for you. There was a woman sitting behind a table who looked up and asked if she could help me. "Do you have information about Jewish survivors? I'm trying to find if any of my family might be alive. I asked her." "Sit down; perhaps you can tell me who you are." I began to tell her my story but was so overcome with emotion that I could hardly talk. My crying was uncontrollable. When she realized that I had been in the Auschwitz camp she jumped up and came over and put her arms around me. "We heard that a woman had escaped from there but everyone assumed that she must have died. We know that the Germans never found her. Can you be the escaped prisoner? Where have you been hiding?" She registered me on her data sheet so I could be found by anyone looking for me. She then told me to go to a house that had been set up for survivors where I could stay until I figured out what I was going to do.

I went back to the Jewish Center the next day to review their lists of people who had returned to Krakow. Jake's name was not there. Neither was Eliza's. In fact I did not see the name of anyone I had known prior to the war. I was truly alone in the world. No one seemed to know anything about the fate of men in the Polish army. There were rumors about many had been taken to Russian prison camps. There were also rumors that many of them had been shot. Thus far no one who had been in the army had returned. Or at least they had not identified that they had been in the army. Perhaps some of them had escaped and blended into the population.

My life in Krakow was getting settled. I found a job working in the Jewish center as a clerk. It paid a small salary but was enough to live on. I found out that the activities of the Center were being financed by a Jewish group from America. It seemed that money was coming from the Polish government in Britain.

Slowly I getting acquainted with other Jewish survivors. Each had a story to tell of how they had been hidden or how they had been able to blend into the Christian population and escape imprisonment. I did not find anyone who had been in Auschwitz.

I soon found that life under the Russians was not much better than it had been under the German occupation. They were just as cruel to the Polish people as the Germans had been. Food was still scarce. I spent hours everyday just searching for something to make a simple soup. Sometimes I could find some bread to go with it but often by the time I got to the head of the line at the bakery it was all gone. And there was an undercurrent of Jewish hatred that many of us experienced. It was dangerous to be out on the street after dark. I heard stories of Jews being beaten by gangs of young boys.

I went back to the center at least once a week to see if there was any new information. One day a man approached me. "Were you in Auschwitz? I heard that you are trying to find Eliza Simonova." I was startled. How would he know Eliza? "While I was in Auschwitz I worked with Eliza in the clothes sorting area for a short time. I was there when her friend Sophie disappeared. She was very distraught about the loss of Sophie, sure that she had died in the snow storm the night of her disappearance. We stayed in contact after that. We were both alone in the world and needed each other to find the strength to keep fighting to stay alive."

I was overwhelmed by meeting someone who knew Eliza. I told him: "'I'm Sophie!" "You're who? You're Sophie? How?, I don't understand. We were all sure that you had died when the guards were unable to find you." We sat down at a table in the center and began to share our experiences. He told me his name was Joseph. While I thought that he was an old man, it turned out that he was only 29. His life in the camp had aged him so much. His hair was gone and the skin on his body hung over his skeleton like a loose bag. He walked with a limp that he said resulted from a beating from a guard.

I was so happy to meet someone who knew Eliza. His news that she had managed to stay alive until the camp was evacuated was overwhelming. Perhaps there was hope that she could still be alive. He told me that he had been at the camp when the Russians were approaching. Everyone had been ordered to line up to begin a march out of camp but he managed to avoid the march by hiding out in the hospital He told me that he had tried to find Eliza so she could hide with him but he was too late to keep her from the march. Eliza was with the group who were sent out of the camp and were forced to start walking west. "I don't know what happened to her, but she was alive when I last saw her."

So Eliza had stayed alive until the end. But what happened after leaving the camp? No one seemed to know the fate of these prisoners. Where did the Germans take them? And there was no way to find out because no one was willing to go into the area still controlled by the Germans. So for now I would have to live with a hope that somehow Eliza may still be living.

In the refugee house I met other survivors. Each had a story to tell: some had lived in the forest with resistance workers, some had been hidden by Christian Poles. Each of us was still hoping that somehow we would find family members who had also survived. We were an odd group of people. Some had lost so much weight that they looked like skeletons. That was how I had looked when in the camp at Auschwitz. Even thought food was scarce at the convent we managed to have soup with vegetables and sometimes meat at least twice a day. I realized how extraordinarily fortunate I was. I had shelter from the cold, warm food to eat, and a loving community to interact with. I had even been able to regain some of the weight I had lost while in the camp.

In the evening the residents of the Refugee House met in a small room off the dining area to listen to the BBC broadcast. All through that spring we were able to follow the advance of the Allied troops into Germany with the end of the war near. With the end of the war in sight, we talked often about what to do. Should we stay here in Poland with the Russian occupation becoming more oppressive or should we try to move westward. Where should we go? Some were talking about trying to get to Israel, others said that perhaps somewhere in South America might be possible. I talked with Joseph about I should do. Where would be a good place to look for Jake. Joseph wanted to go west towards Germany to look for Eliza to see if perhaps she had survived the march out of Auschwitz. He had heard that even though it was brutal, some survived. But we could not go west until Germany was defeated and the war was over.

One afternoon walking home from work, I saw Joseph running towards me. "News," he shouted. "I just heard that there are some Polish prisoners of war who are fighting with the Russians as they are approaching Berlin. Somehow they have survived and are part of the invasion forces in Germany. It might be possible that Jake could be with them. They were part of the force that fought in Warsaw and drove the Germans out." "What, are you sure this is really true?" I asked. Could it be possible that somehow Jake had survived a prison camp and was now somewhere in the Russian army? There was no way to find out but for the first time in years I had a glimmer of hope that Jake could still be alive.

April came with signs of new life, spring flowers were blooming and the air felt warm. People were planting vegetable gardens in areas that had been cleared of the rubble from the Russian advances into Krakow. Even if the houses were no longer remaining, there was hope that food would become more plentiful. I helped plant a small garden next to the refugee house. We could already taste the cabbage and onions that would grow there.

The news of the war was also exciting. Russian troops were approaching Berlin. We heard of some concentration camps being liberated. Dachau near Munich was liberated. This was especially exciting to Joseph who believed that some of the prisoners from Auschwitz were taken there. Perhaps Eliza might be there. His excitement was contagious. He began to make plans to leave for Munich and wanted me to go with him. With the news that some Polish POW's were with the Russian army and headed for Germany, I thought that might be a possible place to search for Jake. Certainly there had been no word of any one returning to Krakow from Russia. And life under Russian control was becoming more difficult.

We woke to great celebrating on May 8th. Germany was defeated. The Russian troops in Krakow were blaring the news from their jeeps as they traveled the city streets. The people were gathering in front of shops that had radios playing. We all rushed out to be part of the celebrating crowd. I found Joseph running down the street towards my house. "It's over" he shouted and caught me and swung me around. "Lets go look for Eliza and Jake."

# CHAPTER 6

# Eliza

The morning roll call ended quickly. Our Kapo ordered us back to our barracks and told us that we were leaving the camp. Eliza did not know what to do. How could she contact her friend Joseph to see what he planned to do about the order. They had talked about the possibility that the camp would be evacuated as the Russian Army was moving closer. But finding him now was not possible. They were all forced into a line and marched to the camp gate. This was it! I was leaving the prison camp to an unknown future. What would happen next?

It was a cold clear day in January as we were preparing to march out of camp. We had nothing with us except the clothes we were wearing. After almost two years as a prisoner in the Birkenau camp of Auschwitz we were about to walk out of those gates. We had no idea about where we were going. We could hear the guns in the distance and knew that the battle between the Russian forces and our German captors was coming near. Was it better to try to hide somewhere and stay in the camp waiting to be liberated by the Russians or to start out with the Germans. Actually I had no choice. We were taken directly to the gate near the entrance of the camp. We had guards along side of us as well as in the front and back of the line. What bothered me most was that I was not able to see my friend Joseph in the men's line. Was he not with us?

The weather was raw and cold. I had a warm coat and good boots that I had taken from the clothing store where I had been working. Many others in the line were not so fortunate and the cold was more than many of them could survive in. The pace of the march was brisk. Many around me were not able to keep up. But if you fell behind, the guards shot you and were left along the side of the road. From the position of the sun we knew we were marching west.

When we stopped for food and water later that day, some of the women with me were able to move off into the woods and disappeared. I was too close to the middle of the group to follow them. Besides, I really wanted to find out if Joseph was somewhere in the march. I wondered if the women who had escaped from the march found safety with the peasants in the area. At this late stage in the war would people still be able to turn a Jew in and get a reward from the Germans? Should I try to escape or stay here to see what would happen next?

Every time we stopped and could talk with the other prisoners, I asked about Joseph. No one remembered seeing him the morning we left camp. He had been at roll call but then disappeared. It became clear that he was not on the march. My despair grew greater. I had lost my family, then Sophie, and now Joseph. I truly had no one left in the world who cared about me or what would happen to me. What was the point of going on?

By the third day of the march I developed a blister on my left foot from rubbing on the boot. I had been able to find a stick along the road that I could use to help ease the pressure on my foot and help me keep up with the march. But between the cold, the hunger, and being tired from the pace of the march, I wondered if I could keep going. We were given little to eat, a piece of dry bread in the morning and a cup of thin soup in the evening. Sometimes when we passed through a small village, the people would try to throw bread towards us. Twice when I was on the outside of the line, I was able to catch some. Once it was a whole loaf of fresh bread that I shared with the women walking with me. It was the best bread I had tasted in almost three years.

We marched for four days until reaching Gliwice. There we were loaded into open cattle cars and began a journey farther west. The cold was awful. The snow was falling by that time and we had no protection from it. We struggled to stay together to conserve what little heat we had. We had no food or water during this part of the trip and the hunger was overwhelming. The pain in my left foot from the blister was getting worse. Fortunately I still had the stick I had found along the road and was able to use it to support myself so I could take some of the pressure off of my left foot. After several days travel we reached a camp near Munich – Dachau. There we were herded into wooden barracks. We were each given one small blanket but it was not enough to keep us warm.

Life at this camp was chaotic. I could do little but lay on my bunk as the infection in my leg was spreading upward. It was impossible to clean the wound on my leg. We had no clean water or anything to clean it with. I was barely able to stand up during roll call. Fortunately some of the other women helped me stand during roll call and then brought me some food so I didn't have to stand in that line as well. We were not required to work in this camp. We just stayed in our barracks and waited for what would happen next.

This was not a "work" camp. It was clear that the Germans had no idea of what to do with us. From the gossip in the camp we learned that the American forces were closing in on the area. The thought that kept many of us going was that this would soon be over. There was no longer any place that our captors could force us to move. With the allied forces coming from the west and the Russians from the East, the Germans were hedged in.

I lost track of time there but at some point I was taken to the "hospital" there at the prison camp. My leg was red and swollen from the infection and I was no longer able to stand on it. I don't know how long I was there but the pain in my leg was getting unbearable. Most days a person would bring us some food but I was not able to eat it. I could no longer sit up to feed myself. I knew that I would finally die from starvation. But I no longer cared. One day I realized I had not seen any of the staff. We had not been fed or taken to the bathroom. Had we been deserted? I slipped in and out of consciousness not aware of my surroundings.

Suddenly I heard some strange voices. They were men's voices talking in some language I had never heard before. A man burst into my room, took one look at my leg and called for something. Two other men came rushing in and lifted me unto a stretcher and carried me out to a vehicle. There were several other prisoners in the vehicle as well and we started off rapidly. Someone put a needle into my arm and soon the pain was lessened.

When I woke up I was in a clean bed in what looked like a hospital. There were several men around me in white coats looking at my leg. There was a needle in my arm attached to tubing coming from a bag hanging above me. I could not understand what the men were saying to me. but finally someone said said "Polski?" 'Ya".

A woman came over to my bed and started talking to me in Polish. She told me that I was in an American field hospital and that I had been rescued from Dachau. I had a very bad infection in my leg that the doctors were trying to treat. She asked me what my name was and where I had been living prior to the war. She wanted to know if I had any family with me at the prison camp who they might try to contact. "No, I had no friends or family left. Everyone was gone."

The days melted into each other. The pain medicine I was given kept me mostly asleep. A nurse came in many times during the day to give me some soup and tea. I had so little strength that someone had to feed me. She insisted that I must eat something but I could only tolerate a small amount at a time. I was finally warm under the blankets on my bed after being cold for so long. The pain in my leg was less because of the medication I was given.

I had been there more than two weeks when the doctor came in with Rosa, the Polish speaking woman. They told me that the infection in my leg was not responding to treatment and they were concerned that the infection would spread to my whole body. If this happened

I would die of the infection. Who would care if I died? I thought. I had faced death so many times since this war began. Why would these people care?

The doctors told me that they thought the best action was to amputate my leg below the knee. I should think about this and ask questions about what would happen to me, Rosa stayed with me to talk about my decision. She told me that in America it was possible to get what she called a prosthesis attached to where my leg would be amputated and I could learn to walk again. She told me that some Jewish group had sponsored other people to go to America to get treatment. This would all take time but it was possible. I thought about what to do for the rest of the day. With no family or loved ones still alive, what was the point of living? The loss of Sophie was unbearable. She was my hope for living when in the ghetto and in the prison camp. Then I also thought about Joseph. He had been so supportive to me as I grieved the loss of Sophie. But now both of them were gone! The courage I had that had kept me going thus far was gone. The easiest way would be to let the infection take my life. But from somewhere inside of me the will to live survived. Even though I saw no hope for the future, I decided to let the doctors amputate my leg. Perhaps I would not survive the operation.

Several days later I was transferred to a hospital in Munich and had the surgery done. My recovery from the surgery was slow because I was still so weak. I still had pain in what had been my leg. How could this be? My leg was gone. The nurses explained about what they called "phantom pain". My nerves were still irritated from the surgery and thought the pain was coming from my leg. They told me that this would get better in time.

One day I was finally strong enough to be lifted into a wheelchair and sit up for a short time. I was learning how to pull myself up when in bed using a bar over my bed. The wound at the stump where my leg had been amputated was very slow in healing because I had been starved so long. I would have to stay in the hospital until it healed. I wondered how I would ever learn to walk again.

Finally the day came when my stump was healed and I was transferred to what the Rosa called a "convalescent hospital." There I would start the slow process of learning to walk with crutches. This was going to take me months because I was so weak.

In the convalescent hospital I was able to communicate with some of the nurses with my limited German. I was gradually learning about my surroundings. I was in what they called the "American" sector. The American army was in charge here. Rosa told me how lucky I was to be here because the Americans were taking care of the Jewish ex prisoners. She told me that back in the Russian sector life was more difficult. I wondered if Joseph had survived the Auschwitz camp and was somewhere in Poland under Russian control. But I would probably never know what happened to him. I was alone in the world and had a future that might mean going to America to get a new leg. I decided to spend my time here at the convalescent hospital learning a little English in case the miracle of going to America might happen.

Every day I went to the physical therapy room to practice walking. I started on what they called parallel bars that I could hold onto as I hopped on my right leg. Then they gave me some crutches to use instead of the bars. I don't know how many times I fell before I was able to walk even a few feet. Learning to walk again would be a slow process.

# CHAPTER 7

# Moving Westward

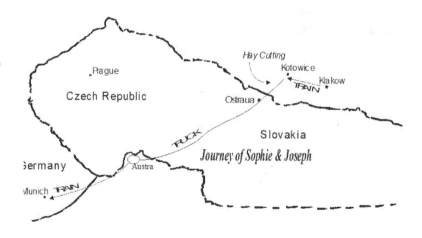

Life in Krakow was becoming more difficult for Sophie and Joseph. There were reports of Jews being beaten by groups of young Poles. It seemed that the hatred towards the Jews was as strong as ever. The city was in ruins. It felt like the oppression from the Russian occupiers was getting harsher. And nothing was left there for them. They had lost family, homes, and friends. They had no hope of finding either Eliza or Jake in Poland.

They decided that they should try to get to the west rather than stay in Poland under Russian control, but the problem was how to do it. Travel permits were required to move about in Poland and they did not know how to get them.

Joseph was in contact with friends from the Polish underground who knew of ways to get across the border into Czechoslovakia, but it required money. From there they thought they could get to Austria and then into Germany. Finding work in Krakow that paid enough to pay the smugglers to get them out of Poland seemed impossible. You needed some type of work permit to get a job.

Their first move was to go west to Katowice where they were not known and could find jobs in the larger city where work papers were often not required. They met at the train station in Krakow late one night and managed to get aboard a train going west undetected. Sophie hid in a bathroom on the train until the conductor had passed through the car and it was safe to enter the main compartment. There were no seats but she found a place where she could put her small bag down and sit on it. Joseph kept moving from car to car managing to avoid the conductor. They made no contact with each other until they reached Katowice several hours later. There they left the train and managed to get behind the station without being detected. So their first move westward was successful.

Joseph had been given the name of a contact in Katowice who would help them find work and lodging. Even though it was late at night they were able to find the contact's apartment and found shelter for the night. Sophie found a job at a restaurant washing dishes. The pay was minimal but the owner asked no questions. Joseph was able to get work by the day as a gardener again with no questions asked. They were able to live in an apartment with three other people who were also looking for ways to get to the West.

It took two months of working in Katowice to gather enough money to pay the smugglers to get them out of Poland. It seemed ironic to them that after their experiences with the Nazi Germans for the past five years that they were so intent to go to Germany. But everything had changed. From the reports they were getting, the Allied troops in Germany, now in charge of part of the country, were treating the Jews who managed to get there very well.

In early September they heard from the smugglers that a group was being organized to start the trip to Germany. The people interested were to meet the next Sunday evening in the woods on the west side of the city. They were to take only one change of clothing and bring the money for the trip. Sophie and Joseph pooled the money they had earned and found it enough to be able to join the group.

"This is it" said Joseph. "Let's go". Sophie was more hesitant. Was she ready to leave her homeland behind? What would be there in Germany for her? Was this going to take her farther away from finding Jake? Joseph was determined to go. He could not rest until he found out if Eliza had survived the march out of Auschwitz. He had lost everything in Poland. His family was gone. His home was gone. The only person left for him was Eliza. He had to find out if she was still alive. He realized that she was the person he loved. Getting to Germany was his only hope for the future.

Sophie spent some very restless nights trying to decide if she should go. She had no hope of finding Jake there. How could he have survived the war and gotten to Germany? Yet she had found no trace of him in Poland. There was such a slight chance that somehow he had been part of the Polish Army fighting with the Russians. Could he have possibly been part of the Polish troops that fought all the way to Berlin with the Russian Army? How could a Jew have been able to join such a force? One day she was ready to go, the next day she thought the idea was impossible. Yet her own story was also impossible. How was she able to escape Auschwitz, find refuge in a Convent, and then meet up with Joseph who was a friend of Eliza? She had to take the chance. So on Sunday evening she left with Joseph to meet the smugglers in the woods as directed.

As each person met the smuggler, a scythe was handed to them and they were told that would become day laborers to help with the hay harvest. In this way they would make their way towards the border with Czechoslovakia. The climbed into a farm wagon and set off to their first assignment. They spent the day helping with the hay harvest. Their food was supplied by the farmers whose fields they were working in and were able to sleep in barns at night. The work was hard but nothing like they had experienced in the prison camp. They worked out in the hot sun but always had fresh water to drink. After a few days of the work, they became accustomed to the rhythm of the scythe and were able to keep up with the other peasants. The best part of the work was that they were ignored by the Russian troops in the area. They fit right with the peasants and their identity was not questioned. Every two days they would move on to a new farm always farther south. It seemed like a perfect cover for their escape.

Some of their fellow refugees became angry about being used as farm laborers when they had paid the smugglers to get them out of the country. They threatened to walk away if they were not taken directly to the border. Joseph and Sophie were puzzled about what to do. Should they believe that the smugglers were going to do as they had promised? "Let's give it another week" said Joseph. "We don't really know where we are. We may be closer to the border than we think." So they continued their pattern of working in a field for several days and then moving on.

Finally one day they worked in a field that that was next to a road that led directly to a border crossing into Czechoslovakia. Guards were stationed on both sides of the crossing. What was the plan now? The excitement among the refugees grew as the day went on. They were so close to freedom but didn't see how they would get across the border with the guards there. But they noticed that the local people seemed to be able to cross without any difficulty. That evening after they had eaten, their smuggler led them into a woods that was behind the hay field they had been working in. There they followed a path that ran behind a red brick farm house. The smuggler told them that the house was right on the border with Czechoslovakia just north west of the city of Ostrava. So this was it. They were about to really get out of Poland. They were led down a path far behind the house and got to a barbed wire fence. It seemed that no one was anywhere near this spot. The smuggler cut a wire in the fence and Joseph helped Sophie through the hole and then followed right behind. They were in Czechoslovakia. The days of hard work in the hay harvest had been worthwhile after all.

On the Czech side they followed a path that led them to a road where a black truck was hidden. There the smuggler gave each of them new identity papers stating that they were Czech citizens with authorization to work in Austria as farm laborers. He wished them well on their journey and disappeared into the darkness. Joseph and Sophie climbed into the truck and relaxed for the first time since leaving Krakow. They were away from the intense Russian presence they had found in Poland. Here the Russian presence seemed much less restrictive.

Their trip south was uneventful; they were in just one of many trucks on the road. It took two days to reach the Austrian border near a small town of Laa. Just before reaching the border the truck stopped to let them out. There they were directed to join a group of peasants who were walking toward a border crossing. In their peasant clothing they fit right in. The guards scarcely looked at them at the border and they crossed without difficulty. Here in Austria the sky looked bluer, the leaves on the trees looked greener. They found that they were in the area controlled by the Allied forces. From the little news they had been able to get back in Poland, this should be good.

Joseph pulled out a map of Austria he had taken with him and mapped out the towns they would travel to. Taking local trains seemed like the best way not to arouse suspicion about who they were or where they were going. They walked into Laa and were able to buy some food at the local market using the German they had learned while in the concentration camp. The train station was there in the center of town and no questions were asked when they bought their train ticket. It seemed that travel here was going to be easy. In this way they made their way west towards Munich.

As they reached Munich they began to see the utter destruction of the city. The train station was just a bombed out ruin. The buildings in the area of the train station were uninhabitable. The enormity of what the war had done was overwhelming. Was this a good idea to have come here? Where to go now? They found a Red Cross table at a shelter across from the train station where they got directions to a refugee center where they could get help in finding a place to live. There they were interviewed and assigned to a Displaced Person's camp just outside the city that provided housing as well as food. They found the tram line that went in the direction of the camp and were able to get to the displaced persons camp. They were assigned to a dormitory and directed to a food kitchen where they had their first real meal in days. The best part of the camp was to be able to bathe and get clean clothes after weeks of traveling and working in farm fields.

They returned to the refugee center the next day where there were lists of people who had made it to Munich. Unfortunately the lists were very disorganized and they realized that it would take several days of searching before they were able to review all the information there. But after days of searching they had to accept the fact that Eliza's name was not on any of the lists. Their discouragement was overwhelming as they returned to the displaced person's camp with no idea of what to do next.

Back at the Displaced Person's camp they talked with every person at the displaced persons camp they met hoping to get information from people who had been in Auschwitz and had made it to Munich. Most of the refugees thought that their search was futile because very few people had survived the march out of Auschwitz.

One day a woman approached Sophie and said she had heard that she was looking for prisoners from Auschwitz who had made it to Dachau. She told Sophie that there was a woman in her unit who had been in Auschwitz and offered to take her to meet the woman. The woman from Auschwitz told her that someone called Eliza had been on the death march and had made it to Dachau. She had a very bad leg infection that started with a blister on her foot and spread upwards on her leg. She was having trouble even standing and had been taken to the hospital ward at the Dachau prison camp. The woman had no idea what had happened to her after that.

Sophie ran to the men's camp looking for Joseph with this little bit of news. Was it possible that this Eliza was who they were looking for? And now how would they begin a search? Joseph suggested that they start with the lists of prisoners who had been rescued from Dachau. This might be more specific than the general lists they had been looking at. So the next day they returned to Munich to continue the search. The clerk at the Jewish Center gave them the list of prisoners rescued from Dachau but Eliza's name was not on it.

They went back to the clerk asking if there was any other information about people who may have been at Dachau but she did not know of any. Disappointed they started out of the center to return to the displaced person's camp. But before going back they stopped at a little café to get some coffee and think about what to do next. There was a group of American soldiers in the café who greeted them and offered to buy them coffee. One of them asked "are you Polish?" "Yes", and he started talking to us in broken Polish. He told us he was from a Polish family and had learned some of the language from his grandparents. He wanted to know where we were from and what we were doing in Munich. He asked if we were Jews. To our surprise he told us that he was also Jewish. What was this? A Jew was part of the American army? What kind of a country was America? Could it be possible that somehow we could go to a country like that where Jews were allowed to live with freedom.

We told him of our search for a friend who we thought might have been in Dachau when the camp was liberated but had not found her name on the lists that had been collected thus far. Shy may have been in the hospital there when the camp was liberated. He asked "have you searched the hospital lists? They were separate from the lists of people rescued from Dachau. Some of the prisoners who were in the hospital unit at Dachau were taken to a field hospital and many of them were not identified at first because they were unconscious and could not respond to questions." He gave us the address of the field hospital and suggested we go there.

The next morning we started out for the field hospital. It was on the outskirts of Munich and was a long walk from the trolley line. It was noon before we got there. At the office we inquired if a person Eliza Simonova was there. After a long wait the clerk came back and said "yes, we had a patient by that name. She had a badly infected leg wound that we were unable to treat. She was sent to the Municipal Hospital in Munich with the expectation she needed to have her leg amputated." Joseph and I were overwhelmed with this news. Perhaps Eliza was alive. The clerk cautioned us that she was very sick when she left the field hospital and the surgery was risky. We should not get our hopes up.

Early the next morning we set off for Munich again to find the Municipal hospital. Once again we talked with a clerk who went to check the records. I could hardly breath while waiting. Joseph could not sit still pacing the long hallway outside of the office frantically. After a long wait the clerk returned and told us "Yes, Eliza Simonova was here, had a leg amputation, and was sent to a convalescent center. She gave us the address of the center. The trail was getting closer.

It was getting late in the day, but we could not stop now. It was close to evening before we found the center. The main office was closed but we would not leave before finding out if Eliza was here. A young janitor came along and asked what we wanted. He told us that there was an Eliza Simonova here and we could find her in the second room on the next hallway. We were running by that time and got to the door. Who would open it? At the last minute we were both afraid that once again we would be bitterly disappointed. Joseph finally opened the door and looked. There was a woman who looked like Eliza but was so changed we could not be sure. She saw us and screamed "Joseph, Sophie. Is it you? How did you get here? Is this possible"? We enveloped Eliza in our arms and were all crying. A nurse came running to find out what all the commotion was about. We were told that it was too late for visiting and that we had to leave. We could not share our stories. They would have to wait for the next day.

Joseph and I returned to the displaced persons camp that evening with the promise that we would be back early the next morning. We were both so excited that we could hardly sit still on the trolley car.

Finding Eliza was a miracle. Could it be possible that I could also find Jake? That might not be as easy as this search was. If he was alive he would probably be somewhere in the Russian held area. Could I go back there after struggling to get this far into the American sector?

# CHAPTER 8

# Reunion

Sophie and Joseph returned to the convalescent hospital the next day. Eliza was sitting up in her wheelchair waiting for them. "I was not sure you were really here last evening – perhaps I had just dreamed this" she exclaimed! "I have so much I need to know – Joseph, what happened to you, where were you when we were marched out of Auschwitz? And Sophie, what happened to you? How did you escape? I know the snow made your walk back to camp that night difficult. But how did you survive"? It was time for Eliza to go to her Physical Therapy session so the questions had to wait. We went with her and watched as she struggled to take a step. She was still so weak! Her body had been devastated by her imprisonment and the death march.

After lunch we put her in the wheelchair and took her outside. It was beautiful clear October day - the sky was so blue – and the mountains in the distance were majestic. Eliza started to cry - "I can't believe that I am alive to see this. I've forgotten how beautiful the world can be!" Sophie said "that's just how I felt the day I was free to leave the convent. I had not been outside for so long that I felt that I had walked into a different world!" "Convent?" exclaimed Eliza. "What are you talking about?" So Sophie told her about her escape from Auschwitz, hiding in the tree cave, being found by Pietre, and hidden by Sister Anna and the other nuns. "We have so much to tell each other but Eliza, you are tired. We need to take you back to your room so you can rest. We'll be back tomorrow and talk more". "No" exclaimed Eliza. "I have to know how you two got together. How did you meet?"

Joseph started to explain what had happened to him at the time the camp was being evacuated. "I hid in the hospital when the guards were rounding everyone up. I stayed there until the Russians arrived to liberate the camp. When it was safe I left the camp but had with no idea of where to go or what to do. As I was walking along the road some men came up to me and said that they were Polish partisans and wanted to help me. Could I trust them? I decided I had no choice so I went with them. They gave me some clothes to wear and food to eat. I stayed with them for several weeks as I regained my strength. I finally decided that I should go back to Krakow to see if any one I knew had survived." But Eliza exclaimed "You didn't know Sophie. What brought you together?" Joseph said, "I heard there was a woman looking for Eliza Simonova. I went to the Refugee Center to see if I could find out who she was. There I met Sophie and heard her story."

Joseph and Sophie saw how weak Eliza was and realized that the excitement of being reunited with them was almost more than her frail body could manage. It was going to take time and good food for her to regain some strength. Right now she needed rest. It was going to take many conversations for us to share how each of us ended up in Munich!

We returned to the convalescent hospital every day and helped Eliza in the physical therapy center. Each day she seemed more sure of herself and was walking longer distances. The nurses told us that she was a changed person since we had found each other. Her will to work at her rehab was so much more than it had been and she was eating more. She now had reason to live.

One afternoon we were sitting and reflecting on our lives. Here we were – three ex prisoners from Auschwitz. How had we survived when so many had died! Joseph asked "What do each of you owe your life to? For me it was a smelly closet filled with decaying mattresses. When the guards opened the door to the closet where I was hiding, they took one look, smelled it, and quickly slammed it shut. They never looked far enough to find me. I stayed there until I heard the Russians out in the hallway and knew it was safe to leave.". Sophie said "for me it was a snowstorm that allowed me to escape and of course Sister Anna who risked her life and that of the other nuns to keep me hidden in the convent." Eliza was quiet for several moments but finally said "for me it was the loaf of bread that someone threw to me on the death march. At my darkest moments I thought about that bread, how good it tasted and that someone cared enough for me to share her bread. I think that was what gave me the courage to keep fighting on when all I could see was despair. And of course after Sophie was lost, it was Joseph who encouraged me to keep going. He kept saying that this war was going to end soon and freedom was near!"

Eliza wanted to know if Sophie had any contact with Sister Anna since she left the convent. "Yes" replied Sophie. "I have written to Sister Anna to let her know that I am in Munich. I told her about finding you. I know that she prays for me everyday, and I know that she is praying that I find out what has happened to Jake."

"If only I had known that you were safe in the convent. You will never know how I almost lost all hope after you disappeared. I was sure you were dead. If it were not for Joseph who kept encouraging me, I would have given up. And then came the march and Joseph was not on it. From there on my life seemed pointless. I almost give up when faced with the amputation of my leg. I don't know where the inner strength came from to make the decision to go ahead with the surgery because at that time my life seemed so hopeless. I am now thankful to be alive and reunited with both of you."

Eliza told us about the possibility of being sent to America to be fitted for a prosthesis. Joseph was very upset about hearing this. He had no intention of being separated from her again. So he said "you will have to marry me so that I can go with you. I don't intend to lose you again." Is that a proposal"? laughed Eliza. "Are you sure you want a wife with only one leg?" "I'll take you just as you are but if you have the opportunity to go to America and get a prosthesis, all the better." "Time for me to leave" said Sophie. "You don't need me here while you work out your life together."

Sophie was happy for Eliza and Joseph but was sad that her life was not working out. At times she wondered why she had survived only to have to accept that Jake had not survived. The news about him was not promising. If only she could get to Berlin to talk with Polish survivors of the Polish Army fighting with the Russians. Perhaps someone knew what happened to Jake. But she was finding that this was looking impossible. The Allies had established tight borders between the various sectors in Germany and travel between them was almost impossible. She didn't know anyone who could help her get the right travel papers.

She went to the Red Cross office in Munich several times a week searching for information about Polish prisoners of war. She finally did find that a Jacob Rosen had been in a German prisoner of war camp in the fall of 1939 but there was no information about what happened to him. He seemed to have disappeared. There was no record of his death or release from the prison camp. It seemed like a dead end.

As Sophie walked the streets of Munich she felt that her life was like the ruined city. Was there any hope for her future? She watched one day as a work crew was cleaning up the rubble from a damaged building. As the rubble was cleared away she was able to see the shape of a new building taking form. Was this a sign for her? Could all of the rubble she was living with now be cleared away and something new take shape? Should she give up on finding Jake and look for a new path for her life? No, she was not ready to give up yet! She needed to know what had happened to him before she could move with her life. She realized that there was little chance that he was still alive. But still she needed to know.

One day after leaving the Red Cross office Sophie ran into the American soldier who had suggested checking at the Field Hospital for information about Eliza. He introduced himself, Paul Sobeleski, and wanted to know if we had any luck in finding our friend. I told him about Eliza, how she had survived the death march out of Auschwitz, about the loss of her leg, and how she and Joseph were going to get married. At that point Sophie broke down crying. "I am so happy for them, but I can't find out anything about my husband. I have lost everyone, my parents, my husband, and now it looks like Eliza and Joseph will be going to America and I have no one left in the world. I'm sorry, I should not be burdening you with my problems.". Paul wanted to know what I had found out about Jake. He said "it's strange that there is no information about what happened to this Jacob Rosen. The Germans kept very good records, the Russians did not. Is it possible that he escaped from the prisoner of war camp? Could that be why the trail seems to have gone cold?" If he escaped would he not have come back to Krakow?" replied Sophie. "Did he die somewhere out in the countryside and is in an unmarked grave? I don't know if I should just give up searching for him and try to get on with my life. But this is not getting us anywhere. Why don't you come with me to meet Eliza. I know Joseph will be happy to see you again".

Sophie and Paul went back to the convalescent hospital: as she knew, Joseph was delighted to see him again. Paul heard each of their stories of how they had survived the war and marveled at the strength each of them had shown in such difficult situations. And thus a friendship that would last a lifetime was begun.

# CHAPTER 9

# Confronting an
# Uncertain Future

Eliza was discharged from the convalescent hospital and came to the displaced persons camp to live with Sophie. Twice a week an American army car drove up to her building to pick her up to take her to physical therapy. What an amazing thing! The idea that she was important enough to the Americans that they were concerned about her progress in walking was almost than she could comprehend. One day she asked the driver why they did this. "Lady, you were badly mistreated in the concentration camp and in being forced to walk miles in the freezing winter. Those Germans are responsible for you losing your leg. We want to do what we can to help you recover. I have a buddy who lost his leg in battle. He is doing just great now with an artificial leg. I hope you do as well."

Eliza heard that he called her a "lady". A lady, not an animal! She had been respected as a person. This was so different from being treated as a "dirty Jew".

These Americans were so different – they made her feel like she had some self worth. After years of being seen as worthless person in the ghetto and the concentration camp, she was beginning to gain some confidence. When she talked about this with Joseph he supported her in her newly gained self confidence. She realized that Joseph had somehow kept his own self sense of worth during the concentration camp experience. This was why he had been so encouraging back at the camp. His optimism had been such a support for her and why she had been so devastated when she realized he was not on the death march with her. Now that he had found her she was ready to face building a new life!

Joseph and Eliza were making plans for their wedding. But were not able to plan for their future life. Should they stay in Germany until they heard about the visas for America or should they be looking for some other country to emigrate to. It seemed that only people who had some connection with a country were getting visas to emigrate but they knew of no family anywhere who could sponsor them. Should Joseph be looking for a job? They could not stay at the displaced persons camp indefinitely. But there were no jobs for a Jewish refugee from Poland in Germany. So until they heard about a possible visa for America their life was in a holding pattern. So they were spending their time participating in an English language class at the DP center.

Sophie did not know what the future held for her. She was not able to make any decision for herself. She did not want to leave Germany until she was able to get closure about Jake. She had to find out if anyone knew what had happened to him. So each conversation with the social workers at the camp ended without a plan for her future. In the meantime she needed to find a way to support herself. There was a class at the DP center to teach typing and she decided to enroll. Perhaps she could find a job in an office somewhere. And even though she had no hope of emigrating to America, she joined Eliza and Joseph in the English language classes.

Joseph was the most optimistic of the three of them about the future. He reminded them of the words of the prophet Jeremiah.

*"for I know the plans I have for you. Plans for your welfare and not evil; to give you a future and a hope"* *Jeremiah 29:11 (NIV).*

Joseph said, I am taking to take this for my motto. God has bought us all to a place of safety and welcome. We have found each other through miracles brought by God." But Sophie objected, "I don't seem to have a future. You and Eliza have a good chance to emigrate to America. I don't have any place to go and I can't make any plans without finding out what has happened to Jake." "But Sophie, think about how God led you to safety at the convent. If the German guards had found you, you would have been killed. Perhaps God has also been watching over Jake as well."

Sophie said "this is easier for you than for me. You and Eliza have each other. You have the hope that you will get visas to go to America. Eliza is recovering from the loss of her leg. Right now I don't even see a way that I can get to Berlin to see if I could find someone who might know what happened to Jake."

"But Sophie think about all that has happened thus far" replied Joseph. "You and I were able to get out of Poland to safety here in the American sector. It was a miracle that we found Eliza. Think of all the good that has come from meeting Paul. Remember the blessing Sister Anna gave you when you left the convent. God will watch over you." "I wish I could be so positive, Joseph. Perhaps with Paul's help I could find out more about the First Polish Army and find someone who may have met Jake and knew what happened to him."

Paul and Sophie met the next day to talk about where to go in their search for Jake. They compared what they knew. Sophie had found that he had been a German prisoner of war but the trail ended there. Paul had learned of a prisoner of war exchange between the Russians and German in 1940 but no Jews were part of it. However Paul wondered if someone had known Jake and might have been part of the First Polish

Army who had fought with the Russians all the way to the battle of Berlin. If only there was a way to get to Berlin and talk with some of the Polish men in the Russian army. He had heard that many of them had been in the prisoner exchange back in 1940 and could have been in the same prisoner of war camp that Jake had been in.

The situation in Berlin was rapidly changing. The administration of the city was being divided into four sectors with the American, British, French joining the Russians in control. Some American troops were being transferred there. Perhaps with some Americans there Paul could find a way to get more information about the Polish forces.

Paul was surprised to get orders to be part of the American occupation force in Berlin. He was to leave Munich in two weeks. But before going he was to gather some staff who spoke Polish and some English. Even though he spoke some Polish, it was not sufficient to carry out his assignment to work with the Polish population in Berlin.

Paul went looking for Sophie as soon as he got the news about his assignment. He wanted to know if Sophie could get a picture of Jake. He suggested that a picture of Jake may be of help in the search for him but Sophie knew that nothing had survived in their home in Krakow. Who could possibly have a picture? Wait, our cook Marie, could she have possibly kept a picture of Jake? Could I get a letter to her? Was she still living in the place where I had met her? Of course, she must still be there. It was worth trying to contact her. Paul and I wrote to her and posted it to the address I had. We told her of our search for Jake and the need for a picture. Paul gave her the address of his unit in Berlin. "We'll see if anything comes of this."

With the news of Paul's leaving Munich, so soon, the wedding plans were rushed forward. Joseph found a Rabbi in the displaced person's camp and the wedding was set for the next week. Paul agreed to be a witness at the wedding along with Sophie. It was not the wedding that Eliza had dreamed of when a young girl but so much had changed in her life that she was happy to at least have a few friends to celebrate with her. Not having her mother there to help her dress and her father to give her away was a great loss. It seemed at times like these the loss of her family was the hardest to accept.

Sophie found a long white dress with long sleeves for Eliza. It needed to be altered because Eliza was so thin but the long sleeves would cover up the hated number from Auschwitz on her arm and the long skirt covered her missing leg.

They were all concerned about to use for the chuppah in the ceremony. They would like to have had a prayer shawl for the covering but that was not possible. No one had anything from their former life in Krakow – family treasures such as this just did not exist. Much to their surprise Paul arrived the day before the wedding with a prayer shawl that the Jewish Army chaplain had given him for a gift to the young couple to start their life together.

The prayer shawl was just what they needed for their chuppah. It was a long Jewish tradition to us it during a wedding. They found four long poles that Joseph attached to the four corners of the shawl. Four of his friends from the DP camp offered to hold up the shawl during the ceremony. They would carry the shawl to the opening where the Rabbi would stand.

The day of the wedding came with a heavy cloud cover and unrelenting rain. But just as the ceremony was to start the sun came out with a beautiful rainbow rising over the camp. Was this a sign that God had not forgotten them? The horrors of the prison camp were behind them and they had a future to look forward to. God had brought them together in a miraculous way and they could move on with their lives.

The chuppah was brought to where the Rabbi was standing and the ceremony began. Paul took the place of Joseph's parents and accompanied him to the chuppah. Sophie did the same for Eliza. Eliza had gained enough confidence in her walking with crutches that she was able to circle Joseph in the traditional manner three times but Joseph stood there with his arms out to catch her if she stumbled. After the Rabbi gave the seven blessings, a glass was brought in a bag and together they stepped on it. Every one shouted Mazel Tov and the party began. Participating in the Jewish traditional marriage here in the displaced persons camp so far from home was bitter sweet. They were so aware of all that they had lost but were thankful for having found each other. Each step forward was part of the healing process. They would never forget the horrors of the concentration camp but their healing process was beginning.

After the wedding Paul approached Sophie with an offer. "I have to take some Polish speaking people with me to Berlin, would you consider being one of them? Now that Eliza is married, you are free to come with me." The offer came as a great surprise to Sophie. "This could be an answer to my prayers, but I hate to leave Eliza behind. What if she goes to America while I'm gone?" She thought here is my chance to search for Jake there. It's not likely I will find anything about him but I have to try. Sophie had many questions about going to Berlin. It would be back under the Russian control that she had worked so hard to get away from. Paul assured her that she would be safe in the American sector; the Russians would have no power over her. Where would she live? There were no services like the Displaced Persons camp in Munich there. She would be on her own to find lodging. Paul assured her that the military would provide for housing for the people he would bring. We would just have to wait to see how it all worked out.

Sophie left the address for Paul's unit with Joseph because they would have to communicate through Paul. Just before leaving they found out that Eliza and Joseph had been approved to go to America so that Eliza could get the prosthesis for her leg. So this was goodbye forever.

The morning Paul and Sophie were to leave for Berlin was cold and rainy, not a good start for the trip. They said their goodbyes to Eliza and Joseph in tears. Paul promised that he would find them in America when he got back home. The hospital that agreed to care for Eliza was in Chicago only an hour or so away from Milwaukee where Paul's family lived. He assured them that his parents would meet them in Chicago and help them get settled in America. So the goodbye for Paul had hope for the future. Sophie had no such hope. She had no way of ever emigrating to America – there was no one to sponsor her.

Sophie climbed into the jeep that Paul had been issued and huddled down under a blanket. The jeep was open to the weather and the raw cold day reminded her of the cold of her days in the concentration camp. She had come along way from those days and at least here she had a blanket to hide under. The other member of the team, he said his name was Grigor, rode along side of Paul in the front. He and Paul kept up a steady conversation but Sophie had no interest in joining in. She was lost in her anxiety – where would this move to Berlin take her? She saw it as the last chance to find out information about Jake. But what if was also a dead end? What would she do with the rest of her life?

The roads were in terrible condition. Hitler's famed autobahn had been badly bombed during the war and potholes were everywhere. They had to detour many times on small country roads through villages that were in shambles. The houses were missing windows and sometimes even roofs. She also noticed that there were no farm animals in the fields. The whole area had been so badly damaged in the war. This was not a country she wanted to stay in but she also knew she did not want to go back to Poland.

The trip took longer than they had anticipated. Between the bad roads and the checkpoints where they had to show their papers it was going to be late at night before they reached Berlin. The checkpoints were easily cleared with Paul's papers showing his new assignment in Berlin. Sophie became aware of how difficult it was to travel in Germany and realized that she would never have been able to get to Berlin on her own. So meeting Paul was so important in her search for Jake. She thought about all of the chance encounters she had that brought her to this moment. Pietre had found her in the tree cave and saved her life. Meeting Joseph who had the contacts with the Resistance leaders led to their escape from Poland. Then Paul provided the information about the field hospital that led them to finding Eliza. Perhaps there might be some encounter in Berlin that would lead her to information about Jake. But were these really chance encounters? She remembered her prayers back hiding in the tree cave. She had asked God for help when she didn't know what to do. Were these chance encounters really God answering her prayer? Certainly Pietre found her because of the vision God gave Sister Anna about the tree cave. He didn't just happen on it! She could not have survived much longer there in the cold. Did she dare ask for help in finding someone who knew Jake. Yes, she would pray again! "Dear God, help me to find someone who knows what happened to Jake." And with that she finally fell asleep.

# CHAPTER 10

# Jake

My call up for the Polish army came in September just shortly after the German invasion. We had known this was coming. I was ready to support my country even though I had left to work in Germany after finishing at the university. We had been living in Berlin but life there had become almost impossible for Jews so two years earlier we had returned to Krakow. Sophie's parents had lived there for their entire life. They feared for our lives because of the news about the repression of Jews in Germany and believed we would be safer in Poland. But all this changed so quickly with the German invasion. So now our fleeing from Germany had done us little good. We were still at their mercy.

Sophie and I did not know what she should do. I thought it would be best if she stayed with her parents both to help them and to give her some comfort. Here in Krakow she had relatives and friends to support her. We agreed to give up our apartment and Sophie would move back to her parent's home. This would only be temporary until I got back.

During our last night together we agreed that if we were separated after this war was over, we would try to leave messages foe each other at the local synagogue. Little did we know what would happen in the coming days. We doubted that our apartment in Berlin would still be ours. The Germans had already appropriated many of the Jews' property there. But at least we hoped that our home in Krakow would still be here.

I was sent to the west of Poland to form a defense against the German invasion but our defenses against the Germans were pitiful. We had horses, they had tanks and airplanes. One of the bright spots of this time was reconnecting with an old school friend Stanislaw Wykowski. We were in the same patrol group and were able to support each other in the face of almost certain defeat by the Germans. We were there only a week before our unit was overrun by the Germans.

On the day we were captured by the Germans we were lined up and told to start walking. We were forced to march in groups of five along a road filled with water from the relentless rain we had over the past several days. If anyone fell by the wayside, he was immediately shot. Stan and I tried to stay together and hold on to each other to keep from falling. The walk was brutal. We had no food and little water. At times I wondered why I was trying to keep up. But the thought of Sophie kept me going. I was determined to find a way to get back to her.

Was there any future for us? All we knew was that we were walking west into German held territory. Several times Polish farmers along the way tried to toss some food to us but we did not get any of it. Being hungry, cold, thirsty and most of all tired was our fate.

That night we reached a prison that was serving as a transit camp with prisoners from many areas. We were packed into small cells meant for two prisoners. However, there were at least five placed in each cell and sometimes more. We had some old buckets of dirty water for drinking. No food was provided that night. However, we did get some dried pieces of bread in the morning. It seemed that that the Germans had no idea of what to do with us.

We were kept in the prison for three days. Then we were lined up outside and were told that we would be marching again to a more permanent camp. As we lined up, we were asked if there were any Jews in the group. One man stepped forward, identified himself as a Jew and was immediately taken out of the line. Stan and I looked at each other and signaled by nodding our heads that we should stay together and I did not admit to being a Jew. For at least at this time, no further inspection was done.

We marched for three days to a more permanent camp. There any Jews who had managed to get this far were identified by other prisoners and separated from the group. We Jews were placed in a hovel – dirt floor, no heat, very little food. We were each issued a thin cotton blanket. The Aryan Polish prisoners were treated a little better than the few Jews who had survived until this time.

Our days were all the same. We lined up in the morning to be counted, given a thin soup to eat and then sent to work outside the camp at a road building project. We were always cold, hungry, and tired. But the lice were the worst. We had no way to keep clean. The Aryan Polish prisoners fared a little better. They were sent to local farms to work where there was the possibility of finding some food left behind after the harvest. I doubt if I could have survived if it had not been for Stan. His assignment was on a dairy farm and was often able to bring back a small piece of cheese and some pieces of good bread. We would meet in the evening and he would share his food with me.

In March of the next year (1940) there was a rumor of a prisoner exchange between the Germans and the Russians. Stan found out that there would be no Jews allowed in the exchange. The thought of being separated from him was more than I could endure. I could not have survived the winter without his help. Late that night Stan and I met in our usual place. He told me not to report for my work detail the next day. I was to be sick and stay behind in the barracks. Early the next morning after the prisoner count, he appeared at the edge of our field and motioned me to come over. He had some papers that had belonged to a man in his unit who had just died. He told me to report to the lineup for the prisoner exchange with the papers. I was now Henryk Tuchani, an Aryan Pole. Jacob Rosen no longer existed.

As the prisoners were lining up to leave the camp there was general bedlam. The Germans in charge were shouting orders that were changed every few minutes. I slipped into a line of prisoners where no one knew me and reported my new name. It was written down by a young soldier without question and I walked towards the field where trucks were waiting to transport us away from the camp. I jumped into a truck where I knew no one and no one seemed to care who else was there. Stan managed to get into the same truck and we were together again.

The trucks moved eastward across the flat plane of Poland. We traveled all day and then into the night. We stopped only once a day so that we could relieve ourselves. There was drinking water brought to the side of the truck but no food. On the second day we reached a Soviet camp and were ordered off the trucks. There we were sent into a shower room to bathe and had our heads shaved to get rid of the lice and were issued clean clothes and boots.

We stayed at the camp for three days not knowing what was to come. We knew we were near the Eastern border of Poland. Some of the prisoners tried to escape but it was futile. We heard the shots and knew they had not been successful. Stan and I decided that life under the Soviets would be better than under the Germans and to wait it out to see what would happen. We could hear the guns. from the battle between the Soviets and the Germans and knew that we would not be here much longer.

On the fifth day the trucks that had brought us to this camp appeared again. We were told to line up and get ready for transport to a new camp. Again we started east father away from Poland. We knew that we were traveling northeast but stayed away from any city that would give us an idea of where we were. As we headed northward, the days were getting longer. It was mid May by now and we had daylight close to 18 hours.

We traveled for over two weeks without any stop always going northward. The ride in the truck was bumpy. We were crowded in so tightly that no one was able to get up to stretch. We tried to get an idea of where we were going by peeking out through a small hole in the canvas covering the back of the truck. The scenery had changed from the flat plains of Poland and the Ukraine to an arid flat expanse with little vegetation. None of us had any idea where this could be. Our only clue was the longer days and the arid vegetation.

We finally arrived at a camp located near the ocean. By this time we had twenty three hours of daylight. One of the men in the truck realized this was the Komi peninsula, a far north section of Russia. The days were fairly warm despite being so far north of the Artic circle because the Gulf stream came this far north and kept the area warmer than one would expect. We were settled into a sparse wooded building with beds three tiers high. In the summer it was warm, but what would the winter bring?

We were assigned the next day to our work sites. Our group was sent to a building site where the structure for a mine was underway. We worked ten hours a day and were fed just twice a day. As long as we were productive our rations were almost adequate. If we missed a day of work, we did not get fed.

We were there in the camp for more than two years. The winters were brutal with the cold wind coming in off the sea. The barracks were poorly constructed and allowed for the wind to come in through the cracks. We tried to fill the cracks with mud from the coast but the nights were still brutally cold. We slept with every piece of clothing we had. The worst part was the total darkness from early November until late February. We walked to work in the dark, worked in the dark, ate in the dark, and then went back to the barracks in the dark. We had no candles even to help with the blackness of the barracks. At least at work we had large search lights covering the area that gave us some sense of a difference between day and night.

Life continued in this way for what seemed like forever. I had trouble believing that anything could change. Many days I thought I should just give up and let myself die. What was the point of struggling on. The one thing that kept me from total despair was the thought that perhaps Sophie was still alive. I had to stay alive so that someday I could search for her. I prayed that somehow she was surviving whereever she was. The hardest part was the not knowing. From what we had experienced with the Germans during the early part of the war, I knew that they were being brutal to the Jews in Poland.

We had no contact with the outside world and heard little about how the war was progressing. So we were surprised in the Spring of 1943 to see notices posted around the camp of the formation of a Polish Army to fight with the Russians. Evidently the Russians needed more man power. We were given the option of "volunteering" for a Polish army unit being formed by the Russian army. Stalin needed more men to combat the Germans. So that was our choice! Continue on in the slavelabor camp or join the army. We were afraid of what would happen to us if we refused to join the army. So we "volunteered". Just as suddenly we had been sent to the far north, we were now sent back towards Moscow to train for army duty.

# CHAPTER 11

# The First Polish Army

We arrived at a hastily put together barracks just outside of Moscow to be inducted into the Russian army. So once again I was in the army. I hoped this would go better than my experience in 1939 in the Polish Army fighting the Germans. I signed in as Henryk Tuchani, not Jacob Rosen. It seemed safer to continue using my Aryan name rather than a Jewish name. But I also knew that the name would not save me if captured by the Germans.

While we had been told that this would be a Polish unit, all of our officers were Russian. We felt that we were not quite trusted by the Russians. They just needed us to fill up their ranks and replace the many Russians already killed in the war. But it was an opportunity to fight against the Germans and that was all right with me and it was better than sitting in the prison camp.

We were measured for uniforms that identified us as part of the Polish army – noted by an eagle on our caps. Why they bothered to measure us I don't know. It seemed that one size fit everyone. Fortunately I had lost enough weight during the past several years that I was able to get into the shirt. The pants were far too large, but with a belt they would be okay. Life at the barracks was miserable; the food was bad, sleeping was difficult, the toilet facilities almost non existent, the mosquitoes were everywhere, the days disorganized. It was no different than the prisoner of war camp we had just left. So I was happy to get orders to go to a training site north west of Moscow to learn to drive a truck. I became part of a motor pool.

I had learned to drive a car back in Krakow years ago, but learning to drive a truck was totally different. These Russian made trucks were difficult to maneuver. I really doubted that I would ever master them. But they were better than what we had back in 1939 in our fight against the invading Germans. At least now we had trucks rather than horse carts! My assignment was to carry ammunition to the frontlines of the battle. Driving a truck loaded with ammunition made one very careful. One false move could end in tragedy. My first day out with the truck carrying the ammunition was terrifying. How I made it out to my designated drop off point and back again I will never know.

As the weather turned colder in the fall, driving the truck became more difficult. The motor wouldn't start, the gas line would freeze up, the tires just spun on the ice on the road. We truck drivers had to look out for each other. I was happy to have some other men in the company who knew more about engines then I did and could help me when my truck would not move. Between the cold, not knowing when I would run into some German artillery forces, and the frequent breakdowns of the truck I was always anxious. I dreaded climbing into the truck in the morning and said a prayer of thanksgiving every evening that I made it back to camp.

The battle front moved westward at a slow pace with the Germans not giving up an inch of territory without a bitter fight. By winter we were in the Ukraine area but despite the cold and snow the battle raged on. The Russian forces were giving no respite to the Germans despite the weather. Every day I carried ammunition to the front lines, but was never sure just where the front line was. We would pass pockets of German soldiers who were behind the German line –it seemed that they did not know where the battle line was either. They were the most dangerous to us driving truckloads of ammunition – one hit on the truck could blow up the load of ammunition and that would be the end of the truck and the driver.

This nightmare came to a sudden end. One morning as I was reporting to the motor pool I heard my name called. It was an officer who told me that I was needed to drive a jeep for a general. I went out to the jeep and met the general. He said "are you Henryk"? "Yes", I replied. "Good. My son was a Henryk. He was killed early in the war. You have a name that is dear to me. That's why I requested you". How could I tell him that Henryk was not really my name. What if he knew that I was a Jew; I had to keep up the pretense of being Henryk. And besides I was thankful not to be driving the ammunition truck. So this began my life as a jeep driver for the general.

The battle continued westward all winter. Being at the rear of the battle was a safer place to be, but it was also gruesome. I saw its effects with bodies lying beside the road everywhere. It was a scene that I had to ignore if I was going to be able to concentrate on my driving. I went wherever the general ordered and asked no questions. He was totally concentrated on the progress of the battle.

By June we were approaching Brest on the Polish border and were about to get back to my own country. The engineers quickly built a temporary bridge over the Bug River to replace what the Germans had blown up in their retreat and we crossed over into Poland. We celebrated as we returned "home" but it was short lived. The destruction left by five years of German occupation was everywhere. The farm houses were destroyed, the villages had few buildings left standing, and no crops had been planted in the fields. Worst was the stories we were hearing about what had happened to the Jews. We saw mounds that we were told were mass graves of Jews who had been taken out to the fields and shot. Also we were told that the Jews left had been rounded up and taken to ghettos in the nearby towns. From there they were taken away by train and never heard of again. I had to be very careful not to show my emotions because I could not let anyone know that I was also a Jew. I had to keep my grief to myself. But hearing what had happened in this area could not have been different than elsewhere. What had happened to my family, to Sophie?

Early in the summer my general was called back to Moscow for meetings and I went back to driving a truck. This time I had a new truck supplied by the American forces that was much easier to drive than the old Russian ones. Also this time my assignment was to transport food, mostly cabbage, to the army field kitchens. The irony of transporting cabbage rather than ammunition did not escape me. I told my friends that I was the new kitchen help! Also we were well behind the front line of battle so the danger was much less. But seeing the destruction of everything as the Germans retreated was devastating.

I returned to my jeep driving duties in early July when my general returned. We were getting close to Lublin and a scouting force had gone ahead to check out a report of a death camp, Majdanek, nearby. The general got a radio message that the camp had been found and we needed to go there at once so I sped off in the direction of the camp. I thought I was prepared to see the worst this war could bring. But I was wrong. The site there was heartbreaking. There were still a few prisoners left behind when the Germans abandoned the camp. They were just skeletons, hardly able to stand much less walk. The medics were gathering them up to take them to a field hospital. We walked into the camp and saw the ovens. Piles of ash from bones were everywhere. People had been burned in these ovens. The smell of burned flesh was overwhelming. We found the gas chambers where prisoners had been killed. I looked into one room and saw piles of shoes – just abandoned. I guess the Germans had no use for them. But they had belonged to real people at one time, people who were no longer alive. I was overcome by all that I saw; I collapsed on the ground crying. So this is where all my hopes and dreams died. How many other camps were there just like this? Is this the fate that Sophie faced? How could anyone do this to another person? What kind of beasts were these Germans?

My general found me on the ground crying and said we had to go on. I could not! I could no longer pretend not to be Jewish - my life was over. I told him that I was not Henryk Tuchani, I was Jacob Rosen and these were my people. I told him the whole story of how I had used the assumed name to get out of the German prisoner of war camp so long ago. But now there was no point in pretending to be someone other that I am. "Henryk, Jacob, who ever you are, you have been my driver for many months now and I need you to continue. The best way to get back at these brutes is to drive them all the way back to Germany and defeat them. Giving up now will not bring your people back." He was right, I had to go on, not for myself but to honor all those who had been killed. The world had to learn of this horror and defeating the Germans was the only way this would happen. We returned to the jeep and started forward. Even though I had lost hope that Sophie could have survived the brutality of the Germans, being part of the army to defeat them was my new goal.

We were headed in the direction of Warsaw where we heard about the uprising of the Jews in the ghetto. At least some Jews had fought back. Were there any left in the City? Could we help save some of them? As we approached the Vistula River in October about to reach Warsaw, the troops suddenly stopped. We could hear the guns in the distance and learned that the people in Warsaw had risen up against the Germans occupying the city. We were anxious to join the fight but our orders were to stop. Why? No one knew. Just sitting there listening to the distant battle was agony. Our orders to move forward did not come until January when it appeared that the people in Warsaw had lost their fight against the Germans.

The city we entered was in ruins. There were no bridges left over the Vistula River, the city center was totally destroyed, the people had little food or a place to live. We had to fight hand to hand with the German forces still left in the city. Fortunately most of them had already retreated westward. We soon had the city under our control and began the move westward. It seemed that the Germans had begun to give up the fight. It was so different than what we had experienced in the Ukraine. We moved 170 miles in just nine days. It looked like the German forces were retreating to the German border to regroup there and fight for their homeland. Poland was no longer important to them. Berlin was now in our sights.

We arrived at the Oder River and again halted to prepare for the assault on Berlin. It took almost two months to get the supplies we needed for the final battle in this war. During this time I was driving back and forth to check on supplies coming from the East. We had to rebuild railroad lines so that needed supplies could reach us. And all of the time we had to cope with never ending rain. The Oder River kept rising and we knew this would make our eventual crossing more difficult. But we had no attacks from the Germans who were on the other side of the river. The reports we got about the Allied forces were also encouraging as they were rapidly moving across western Germany. The plan was for the Russian forces to attack Berlin while the Allied forces went farther south. There was concern that if the Allied forces attacked from the west while the Russians attacked from the east there could be confusion and our forces could end up shooting at each other. So the battle for Berlin would be ours.

Finally on April 16, the battle began. We crossed the Oder River without much difficulty but were caught in the mud on the west side. The river had gone over its banks from heavy spring rains and release of water from a reservoir upstream. What a mess! I had all I could do to get the jeep to move through the mud! We were hit with heavy artillery from the Germans as we moved west of the river. They were dug in on a ridge – Seelow Heights about 11 miles beyond the river – and the battle there went on for four days. Finally the Germans retreated and we had an open path to Berlin. Our unit was ordered to turn southwest towards Torgau on the Elbe River. On the drive south we met with little resistance from the Germans. Apparently all of the Germans forces had been ordered to Berlin for the final battle. The bridge at Torgae had been destroyed by the Germans but we were able to cross by boat and meet the American forces on April 25th. And that's where the war ended for me. Back in Berlin the fight went on. On April 29th we heard that Hitler had committed suicide. And on May 2nd the German garrison in Berlin surrendered to the Russian forces. Berlin had fallen.

# CHAPTER 12

# Berlin

## Jake's Story

I was sent to Berlin as part of the occupying forces after Germany had surrendered. The city was so destroyed that I found it hard to make my way around. I went to our old neighborhood to see if the apartment building where we had once lived was still standing. It was not! The main synagogue was so damaged that it was not usable – not that there were any Jews left in the city to worship there anyway. This city is not a place that I wanted to be. However, I had not been discharged from the army so I was here.

One of he first things I did when I go back to Berlin was to check at the First Polish Army headquarters to see if there was any news about my friend Stan. It took two trips back there before I got information about him. He had been part of the invasion force to capture Berlin and survived days of brutal fighting there. But he had been badly injured and was in the hospital recuperating. On my first free day I went to the hospital and found him. He was walking with crutches because of a leg wound and was soon going to be sent back to Poland - no longer of any use to the Russian army! We spent the day sharing our experiences of the last months. We had so much to tell each other. What a miracle we had both survived the brutal fighting.

Stan wanted me to go back to Poland to meet him there when I was released from the Army. But, I did not want to ever go back to Poland. I could not face the loss of my wife and the rest of my family – there was nothing left for me there. So this was good by forever. All I could do was thank Stan for his friendship and help in saving my life from a certain death in that German Prisoner of War camp. We promised to stay in touch. I would be here in Berlin until the Russians decided I was no longer use to them.

As I thought about the grief that I was experiencing facing the loss of my family, I began to think about the family of Henyk Tuchani. Were they looking for him? What if they found that he had been one of the men released from the German Prisoner of War Camp? But of course he was not; rather he had died in the camp. If his family was still alive, they deserved to know of his fate. They needed to know that he was buried in a mass grave there at the camp. I asked Stan to look for his family and tell them of his death.

Our unit was finally given a two week furlough. My friends were all planning to go to Poland to check on their families. They had reason to hope; I did not. So I refused to go with them. I spent my two weeks searching the records that the Germans had kept of the people transported to the camps. They were so efficient! As I went through the records I found the names of my friends, classmates, even my parents. They recorded who was put on each train and where the train was headed for. So it was not surprising that I found Sophie's name on a list for a train headed to Auschwitz. By this time I was so numb to my losses that I did not even cry when I saw her name. I knew what happened at these camps. I had seen the remains of the Majdanek camp. At the document center I was told that some of the prisoners from Auschwitz had been taken to the prison camp Dachau just outside of Munich. The clerk suggested that I look at that list. Sophie's name was not there.

I went back to my barracks and laid on my bed unable to even think. Learning that Sophie had been taken to Auschwitz was not unexpected. I had seen what had happed in northern Poland. Why would it be any different in southern Poland? There was no way she could have survived. My life was over. Why had I survived the prison camps, the fighting, coming back to Berlin. Why could I not have died also?

My friends found me there that evening and wanted me to go with them to eat. I just laid there with my face to the wall and didn't even answer. The next morning was no better. I spent the next few days walking in a daze. What should I do now? I could not stay in Berlin. The memories were too painful. I did not want to go back to Poland. Some of my friends were talking about emigrating to Israel. Should I go with them after we were discharged from the army? Where else was there to go? But for now I was stuck in Berlin until my discharge came through.

## Sophie's Story

We arrived in Berlin in the rain. In just our short drive through the ruined city, the amount of destruction was overwhelming. Most of the buildings were so badly damaged that I wondered how people could live in them. I was assigned to a small hotel that was used to house women associated with the American forces in the western part of the city. It had a roof covering most of it, but many of the windows were blown out and just covered with wood. The stairways were difficult to navigate because some of the slates were missing. I had to be very careful when using them and I did not like to go out of my room after dark for fear of falling if I missed a broken step.

I had heard that the Polish men who had fought with the Russians were in the eastern part of the city. So the next morning after arriving I set off to see if I could find the headquarters for the First Polish Army in the eastern sector. There was only one trolley line running to the eastern sector that went through areas almost completely destroyed. I noticed that there were no young men on the streets except for military personnel. Even the teen aged boys were gone. The women on the streets were like shadows of themselves. They were thin, their clothes were ragged. As they walked in the streets they looked from side to side as if expecting danger at any moment. It seemed that the battle of Berlin had done so much harm to the civilian population. It had not been like this in Munich. As we approached the grounds of the Zoo the extent of the damage was overwhelming. The grounds were so filled with craters from the fighting there that you could not walk through them. The trees along the Unter den Linden were like match sticks. The beautiful city I had once known was gone. Seeing all of this destruction helped me to lessen my hate for the German people. They too had suffered in this terrible war.

I found the headquarters for the First Polish Army and went in. There were soldiers everywhere but I couldn't find anyone who would talk to me. How would I be able to find someone who might have known Jake? I was sent from one office to another in my effort to find someone who had records of who was in the First Polish Army. It seemed no one knew for sure. I was told that they were working on trying to find out who had actually been inducted into the army, who died during the war, and who was presently part of the occupation force in Berlin. It seemed that each unit had its own records and there was no central place that they were kept.

I went back home discouraged and realized I would need to find a new way to carry out my search. The good news when I got back to the office of the American forces was that Paul had received a package from Krakow addressed to me in care of him. I ran to his office but he was not there. He would not be back until the next day. Another day of waiting!. Could it be the picture of Jake that we had requested?

The next morning I met with Paul and opened the package. Yes, it was a picture of Jake! Maria had found a picture taken just shortly before the war broke out. It also included a picture of my parents! I had never hoped for such a gift! Jake's picture may be useful in the search for him unless he had changed so much that there was no longer any resemblance to the picture. But it was worth trying. It seemed that my best chance of finding out if Jake had been part of the Polish Army was meeting someone who had known him. It seemed unlikely that I would but it was my only option at the moment. I could not go on with my life until I had done everything possible to find him.

Paul had a meeting that day with some Polish officers and said he would take the picture with him. I returned to my job in translating Polish war materials into English for the Americans. Perhaps it was safer for Paul to do this because it was really not safe for a woman to be out on the streets alone approaching the Russian soldiers.

The days went on like this. I took the picture of Jake with me when ever I went out of the office. But finding one person among the thousands of Polish army men seemed impossible. I had also gotten a letter from Eliza and Joseph. They were leaving for America in a week! They were hopeful that at some point I would be able to join them there. Perhaps with my job with the American forces would be a way. Some of my friends in Berlin suggested that I should give up on finding Jake and find an American soldier to marry! That would be a ticket to America! But I was not ready for this.

## The Encounter

Jake had gone to his favorite eating place in Berlin for dinner one night. His furlough was over and he was back to the routine of policing a city where he was not wanted. He was still deciding what to do when his discharge came through in a month. Staying in Germany was not an option. From the news he was getting from Poland, returning there was not either. Perhaps at attempt to get to Israel was his best option. But that also was very difficult. He did not know what to do.

Two American army guys sat down at the table next to Jake He could not help but hear their conversation even though he was only able to understand a few of their English words. They were talking about a Polish woman that one of the men knew. One man asked "who is this woman working for you? Why is she here in Berlin?" The other replied "she has an incredible story. She was a prisoner in Auschwitz who managed to escape and was hidden in a Polish convent for more than a year. She managed to get to the west and now is trying to find if her husband survived the war." "And you believe this story? No one ever escaped from Auschwitz" replied the other man. "Yes, the story is true. I have been in contact with Sister Anna, the Mother Superior at the convent and she told me how Sophie had escaped from Auschwitz and how the nuns found her."

My ears picked up when I heard the name Sophie, a prisoner at Auschwitz who escaped! I got up from the table and approached the men. "Excuse me. a woman Sophie escaped from Auschwitz?" My English was so limited that I did not know if they would understand me.

"Polski the man asked? When I replied yes, he switched to Polish. I asked "Do you know where she was from and who is her husband?" And what about an escape from Auschwitz?" He replied "Sophie was living in Krakow when she was taken to Auschwitz. She escaped from the prison camp and was hidden in a convent until the Russians liberated that area of Poland. Her husband had been called up by the Polish Army at the beginning of the war and she's had no news of him since then. It's possible that he was a German prisoner of war but we have not been able to find out what happened after that."

I grabbed the table to help steady myself. Could I believe what he was saying? They both looked at me with wonderment. Why did I look so ashen? Then the first man looked at me again and exclaimed "You're Jake. I recognize you from your picture." "Yes, Sophie is my wife! And you say she is here in Berlin?" I was crying uncontrollably by this time. The two men helped me sit down at the table. The food went uneaten as we tried to process what had just happened. How could a chance meeting in a restaurant bring Sophie and me together? There were so many questions. How could I go from no hope to finding that Sophie was alive?

The man who knew Polish kept looking at me. He said" I don't understand. The name on your uniform is Tuchani. How can you be Jacob Rosen?" I had to explain the whole story about getting out of the

German Prisoner of War camp using an assumed name. He said "no wonder we could not find you! We found a Jacob Rosen who had been captured by the Germans but he seemed to have disappeared. I can't believe that we just happened to meet in this restaurant! We have to take you to Sophie now."

He suggested that I go with them back to the hotel where Sophie was living. He thought he should go to find her first to prepare her for the news that I was alive. We drove through the bombed out streets to the American sector. I was numb. I could hardly process what was happening. To think that somehow Sophie was here in Berlin at the very time I had seen her name on the transport lists. What if I had gone with my friends to Krakow rather than staying here? My chance encounter at the restaurant would never have happened.

Paul went up to her room and told her that she needed to come down to meet a man who knew her. "Some one I know?" she asked. "Here in Berlin? How does this person know me?" "Just come with me" replied Paul. She walked into the lobby and saw Jake – she tentatively whispered "Jake, are you really Jake?

How did Paul find you? You are Jake! I can't believe this." Jake rushed over and held her as she was about to collapse. "Yes, I am Jake. A miracle has happened!"

# EPILOGUE

Eliza and Joseph went to Chicago for Eliza to be fitted with a leg prosthesis. While there they learned that Paul's parent had arranged for their synagogue to sponsor them for immigration status. They moved to Milwaukee when Eliza was discharged from the rehab center where she had learned to walk with the prosthesis. Joseph was offered a job in the clinical laboratory section at Mt Sinai hospital in Milwaukee. The director there worked with him to get his transcripts from Jagiellonian University in Krakow where he had been a chemistry student prior to the war.

Eliza and Joseph's apartment in Milwaukee wa in a Polish neighborhood on the south side. It was just a block from a Catholic church and school that had a large Polish congregation. Eliza walked past the school every day as she practiced using her new leg. She often stopped to watch the children playing. One of the nuns teaching at the school spoke Polish and would greet Eliza with *dzien dobry* (good morning).

One day the nun invited Eliza to come to the convent for coffee, Having someone to talk in Polish with was wonderful! Eliza told her about her friend Sophie and her experience hiding in a convent back in Oswiecim after escaping from Auschwitz prison camp. The nuns were so moved by what Sister Anna and the nuns did in protecting Sophie at the risk of their own lives that they began to correspond with Sister Anna. They organized the children at the Catholic school to gather materials for care packages to send to Sister Anna who then distributed them to children in the community.

Sophie and Jake left Berlin after Jake was discharged from the Russian Army and went to a displaced persons center in Stuttgart hoping to emigrate to America. The wait was long to find a sponsorship for them. While there Jake became aware of the many children in the DP camp whose education had been interrupted by the war. He set up an informal school and enlisted several of the DP's as teachers. In doing this he discovered how much he loved teaching.

While they were in Stuttgart they head from Stan that he had found the family of Henryk Tuchani living in Katowice. Both his wife and parents had survived the war. He had met with them and told them how their son had died in the German prison camp and where he was buried in a mass grave outside the camp. Stan was uncertain how much more to tell them. But they questioned him why he had sought them out just to tell them about their son's death. He finally admitted there was more to the story. He told them that Henryk had developed pneumonia and there was no treatment in the camp. His last hours were very difficult as he struggled to breathe. But he said, there is some good that came out of Henryk's death. 'I don't know how you feel about Jews. But Henryk's death resulted in saving the life of a Jew."

There was complete silence. His father finally said "this is all too much for us to deal with right now. Give us a little time to think about this. Perhaps we can talk later." "Yes" said Stan. "I will come back if you would like to know more of the story."

A week later Henryk's father contacted Stan and said that the family would like to meet with him again. They wanted to know more about the Jew who was saved. Stan went back to Katowice and told them how Jake had gotten out of the prison camp using Henryk's name. And then he told them how Jake had found his wife in a miraculous way after they had both given up hope for either of them surviving the war. Henryk's mother said "I would like to meet Jake. Is he here in Poland?" "No, he is in Germany. I will let him know that you would like to meet him."

Stan wrote to Jake and told him that Henryk's family would like to meet him. This was a crisis for both Jake and Sophie. They did not want to go back to Poland, but yet felt an obligation to try to meet with Henryk's family. Sophie knew how desperate she had been to get information about Jake. Did they owe Henryk's family something for using his name to survive the was? Perhaps they needed to find a way to meet Henryks family before they emigrated to another country. But all attempts for a meeting were not successful. There was no way for Jake and Sophie could get travel documents to go back to Poland. the Tuchani family were not able to get travel documents to go to Germany. So the families never met. But Sophie did write to them and thanked them for the way their son had been used to keep Jake alive.

Back in Milwaukee Eliza and Joseph often talked with their new friends about Sophie and Jake's story and how much they hoped to find a way to bring them to America. One day the priest at the local Catholic church came to visit and surprised them with a proposal. The people at the church had decided that they would sponsor Sophie and Jake. They were working with Catholic Social Services to get approval for them to emigrate to America! They would hire Jake as a math teacher for their high school.

The long awaited day came when Sophie and Jake arrived in Milwaukee. The nuns who befriended Eliza, the church sponsorship committee, and the priest joined Eliza and Joseph at the train station to greet them. This was the final miracle. Eliza and Sophie were again together.

Printed in the United States
By Bookmasters